The DEATH *of* VENICE

A MAGIC REALISM STORY ABOUT THE DECADENCE OF VENICE AND HUMAN INDIFFERENCE

After a bet between two wizards made when Morgana built Venice on magic water, the city is damned to disappearing from the face of the earth. The incompetency of humankind to preserve the city's beauty is threatens its existence. Yet, hope remains to prevent disaster in the form of one college student's love for Venice and its paladins.

The Death of Venice

©2022 Eldo Frezza

print ISBN: 978-1-66787-733-4
ebook ISBN: 978-1-66787-734-1

SUMMARY

How can the indifference and the inability of humankind break even one of the most beautiful spells of this world? The story is set in Venice in a magical city created by a spell of Morgan Le Fey, who, in agreement with Merlin, made a pact to build one of his creations if Man could maintain the city's beauty. Only a philosophy student, Marco, can save Venice from disappearing from this world.

This magic realism story intertwines practical life, excursions among the beauties of the streets of Venice, pollution problems, philosophy, the coexistence of different religions, all during the golden age of Venice. It describes the ineptitude of Italian politicians, the indifference of the inhabitants, and a story of love. A malignant wizard living in a different universe and a Tsunami over the ruin of Venice make this book intriguing. Marco's love for Venice can only be described as obsessive, yielding no room for others to enter his life. Genevieve, a visiting, northern European woman inspired by a love book, searches for love herself in Venice. She interjects into Marco's world, hoping to capture his heart. Will Marco ever be able to love anyone but Venice? Is Marco reliable? Is he going crazy? He's already obsessed with Venice. Perhaps he is crazy, after all. Or maybe this is the reality of this story. Will Marco, the new Venetian paladin, be able to save Venice?

Other books in the genre of Magic Realism. Dream or no dream is the question. I'm a big fan of Jorge Luis Borges. He constantly was playing with these types of ideas. What's more, he would tell you only part of the story, pretending that he didn't know the rest. But once the reader is held captive by the story, they are at the mercy of the character. My book also portrays a realistic picture of life in Venice and its deterioration, with a mix of fantasy like Alexandra Christo's to Kill a Kingdom. In The Death of Venice, the mystic forces come to get the city akin to Sarah Mass's Tower of Dawn. In my novel, the main character meets the Hero of Venice, imprisoned in a sort of hell. Similarly, in Janice Engelhardt's The Finger of God, I share the biblical and mythological connections to life and the historical realm of religion. The romance developed in this book about a secret woman parallel Dante's La Vita Nova and Inferno in Dante's search for his Beatrix.

Author Eldo Frezza is a surgeon and an Italian journalist who was born in Venice, Italy. He moved to the US to practice medicine in 90'ies. Frezza is the author of non-fiction books The Health Care Collapse, Medical Ethics, Professionalism in Medicine, The Business of Medicine. The Death of Venice, a debut novel, features his native city embroiled in supernatural fantasy mixed with magic realism.

This novel was written to bring attention back to Venice
and save this wonderful and magical city.

CONTENTS

The
DEATH
of
VENICE

ELDO FREZZA

PART I

CHAPTER 1

MORGANA MIRAGES

"*My God! Those buildings just crashed down into the water!*"

Marco and Giorgio had been walking in the silent solitude of the night. They'd fallen equally silent among themselves, like Dupin and his narrator on the Paris Street, when the roar rolled over them in a continuous wave of destruction and screams assailed the air.

The buildings were falling apart. Glass rained down and dissolved into the sand on the ground. Screams came from somewhere within the din. The people in the houses were trapped. The wind picked up. Marco's eyes went to the water in front of the Municipal Building of *Ca' Farsetti*. It was the color of sunset. And it was rising.

"Is Venice sinking...?" Giorgio shouted; his voice barely audible. The water was now swallowing the walls, windows, roofs, and people on the opposite side of the *Canal Grande*. "The buildings are disappearing!"

Marco stared in horror and fascination. Venice didn't get earthquakes. Tsunamis too, were non-existent. And yet, something was shaking the earth and swallowing Venice.

Giorgio's hand was stuck to his forehead. "*Madre di Dio,* all of the riverbank is sinking!"

Marco directed his gaze to the opposite side of the Canal Grande, the *Riva del Vin* was almost completely underwater.

Dark shapes moved in the water, bobbing and rolling along the surface like black bubbles. Rats, the size of felines. Marco's stomach lurched. The rats were everywhere. He could no longer distinguish between vermin and water. The primal horror of the scene struck him then: The things were devouring everything edible that had just been disgorged from the drowned houses.

Everything edible. Nauseous horror overtook him, and his stomach lurched again.

Screams came from somewhere—in the houses. Or was this his mind supplying the orchestrations of death for him?

Something incongruent with the scene struck him then. He looked around. The Calles was devoid of people.

Where is everybody?

He swallowed hard, trying to dislodge the brick dust that had caught in the back of his throat. And then, as if his humanity were being tested, he was suddenly seized by the impulse to intervene. He took off, not bothering to look back to see if Giorgio was following him. But Giorgio, being the same runner he had been in high school and then later in college, was next to him, then overtook him by several feet.

They ran on their side of the riverbank toward *Ca Farsetti.* As they approached from the *Calle del Carbon,* they could see now that *Ca Foscari,* the university building on the left, and the *Rialto Bridge* on the right were sharing the same fate as the others.

Sinister shadows glided across the water toward them.

"The rats, they're coming at us!" cried Giorgio.

A voice came out of Heaven, trumpeted by the fifth angel:

"Venice is doomed."

CHAPTER 2

DISCERNING MEANING

"*Signori...? Signori...?* We need to close the theatre."

Marco had been staring at a blank screen for the better part of thirty minutes, vaguely aware that Giorgio was next to him the entire time.

Sometime during the third act of *Le Diavolesse*—Francoise had just begun to make love to some woman, ostensibly to gain possession of a magic tunic—Marco felt a sense of unease overtake him. Intuitively, he knew that Giorgio had felt it too.

Now he sat—awakened, as it were, by Adolpho, the one-eyed projectionist with a grin like a crocodile who'd worked in the *Bei Giorno di Cinema* art house for forty-eight of his seventy-two years on earth.

"I've given one eye and part of a leg to the *Cinema*," he said jovially. "I do not expect its patrons to do the same. Nor does Signor Bologna run a boarding house."

Marco moistened his lips, becoming self-consciously aware of the snap of dryness there. It was then that he also became aware of Giorgio, who was getting up slowly out of his seat, his bones cracking. Neither man spoke to each other or said anything to Adolpho, who limped up the aisle whistling a folk song of which he did not know the name.

They walked out into the late afternoon air beset by the scent of salt.

"Do you want to talk?" Giorgio said, his tone one of understanding.

Marco stopped and turned, shielding his eyes from the sun. "Did we have the same vision?"

"I had a bad dream that the buildings were crashing into the water—"

"Not a dream," Marco said.

"Yes, it was," his friend said after a moment.

"The same dream? And you know exactly what I'm talking about, It—"

"Enough." Giorgio's temper was rising.

"It was a vision."

Giorgio barreled ahead of him.

Marco called after him. "Where are you going? Off to dine alone again?"

His friend stopped and turned, staring, waiting for Marco to catch up. And when he did, Giorgio moved on, determined to get a meal with or without his friend—preferably with.

"Perhaps I overdid it running at St. Helena today," Marco said after a moment.

"Me, too. I went to the gym. And you know me. I was trying to show off. There were some new girls there today."

Marco felt something relax inside him. Like most university students, Giorgio had a keen interest in impressing beautiful girls. While Marco shared some of his friend's enthusiasm for the fairer sex, he was generally more interested in philosophy and journalism. They were both students, sharing nearly all of their classes at *Ca' Foscari*, and had been friends since elementary school.

"We're not talking about it, then?" Marco said after a moment.

"I'm more interested in your opinion on a particular topic."

"Go ahead."

"Was this the best Morgana yet?"

Marco harkened back to the woman of the film—her sumptuous figure and the curve of her hip which was like the head of a viola.

"Or do you prefer the Mediterranean version," Giorgio added, "where Merlin and the sorceress get along all nicely-nice?"

Marco nodded his head slowly, feigning contemplation. "This is a discussion to be had over coffee."

The sun was now setting, and in the purple dark, they walked toward Campo San Bartolomeo for a late snack before heading home.

CHAPTER 3

THE RIALTO BRIDGE

In the Campo, they lingered near the monument to Goldoni.

"What do you think?" said Marco.

"What do I think of what?"

Marco motioned with his chin. "Goldoni."

Giorgio craned his neck to look up at the bronze statue of Venice's most revered writer of comedy. The oxidized patina made a face look sickly in the twilight. Giorgio shrugged. "Never read him."

Marco stared at his friend. "You're joking."

"No."

"I could have sworn you did."

"That was a fantasy of yours."

Marco stroked his chin, looking up at the statue himself as if the answer to the riddle lay there. It must have been a fantasy, for he wanted with all his heart for Giorgio to be a literary man.

The subject of fantasy ignited a small fire in his soul as he now recalled the vision in the *Cinema*.

"What do you think it was?"

"I told you. A fantasy."

"No, the vision in the *Cinema*."

"A dream."

"A dream that we both had," Marco said, raising a finger for emphasis.

"Ok, Marco, how about we play in your philosophy sandbox for a moment? Hm? How do you know I had the same dream?"

"Because you told me you did."

"When?"

Marco looked confusedly at his friend. "Right after we left."

Giorgio had a mischievous smile on his face. "And how sure are you of that?"

"Ah," said Marco, catching Giorgio's amusement, "I see where you're going with this. You want me to explore the nature of memory. You think only one of us was actually dreaming and told the other."

Giorgio patted him on the shoulder. "They say memory is the greatest of all liars."

"So, you're saying we didn't share the same dream."

"Correct. Do you approve of my theory?"

"No."

"And why not?"

"Because it's boring."

Giorgio leaned against the railing surrounding the Goldoni statue and folded his arms. "Okay then. Please give me a more enticing explanation. And please, say nothing of visions."

"Fine," said Marco. "We were watching a Morgana movie, and so I say we were visited upon by a Morgana mirage."

"A Fata Morgana, eh? Aren't those limited to sailors?"

"Not necessarily. The ever-present spirit of Morgana knows how we fancy her, and so was toying with us. To further indulge her playful side, she decided to confuse us with whether it was one or both of us that had the vision."

Giorgio got up and began walking toward the side street.

"Where are you going?" said Marco.

Giorgio turned. "To the Rialto. Listening to you, it's occurred to me that I may still be dreaming. If I can walk across the water, I'll know it is so. If not, I'll dry off and get something to eat. You are, of course, welcome to join me." With this, he turned back and began making his way up the street toward the Rialto footbridge.

It was then that something caught in the corner of Marco's eye, and he turned abruptly toward the statue. It was facing slightly more North than it had been a moment ago. He stared agape.

"Fata Morgana," he said softly.

He went to the side street and called after Giorgio. His friend turned, still walking. Marco motioned him over. Giorgio stopped and stood with his arms on his hips.

His heart racing, Marco turned back to see the statue facing the way it had been all along.

After a moment, he went to join his friend, who had by this time reached the footbridge and was waiting for him.

CHAPTER 4

SOMEONE TO LOVE

They stopped in at the Galleone rotisserie for a warm mozzarella in carrozza. They grabbed it to go, and, having exited the rotisserie, turned into an alleyway crowded with trash: empty plastic bottles, used napkins, dashed cigarettes, and splintered plastic utensils. Disgusted, Marco handed his food to Giorgio and bent down to pick up the refuse.

"They can't even place the trash in the canisters!" he said, tossing the stuff into a bin and wiping his hands on his pants afterward.

Giorgio handed the fried mozzarella back to him. "You're on a mission to save Venice singlehandedly, aren't you?"

"So, what if I am?"

"Shall we head home?"

"The night's still young," said Marco. "What do you say we take the long way towards Saint Mark Square?"

"Are you sure?" said Giorgio. "It's more touristy. There's the possibility we'll encounter more trash. You won't be able to restrain yourself and I'll have to roll you home in a wheelbarrow by the end of it."

Marco smiled as they made their way down the street. To him, there was nothing as magical as walking the narrow *calle*. But in truth, he was still shaken from his visions. He envied Giorgio for his ability to either shake it off or otherwise be satisfied with some other explanation.

But in time, he relaxed, for with each trip down the *calle*, Venice revealed a secret he hadn't seen the last time—a new play of light on a building, or the way two buildings seemed to interact as neighbors. In her slowly revealed mystery, Venice was truly beautiful.

"Look at this bridge," Marco said, pointing at the Rialto, in particular to a young couple at its apex, kissing in nighttime silhouette. "I wonder how many wars, secrets, and kisses have been witnessed by this bridge through the years."

Giorgio laughed gently. "Don't worry, my friend. One day you and beauty will give this bridge something to remember, I am sure. Or at least something to think about."

Was it part of the vision now, or had the couple dissolved into the mist of night at their approach? Marco decided not to ask his friend if the vision was shared.

"One thing is sure," he said instead, "I would never be able to go out with someone like your last girlfriend. Whenever that woman opened her mouth, I wanted to run and hide."

"Okay, okay," conceded Giorgio. "Probably not the smartest girl, but I was fine with her."

"She could go on for hours. Talking, that is. She talked way too much for one human."

Giorgio punched his friend's arm. "I guess you don't like competition, eh?"

They walked home on the warm, humid night. Most nights the streets were thronged with tourists, but tonight, Venice was almost deserted. Only a few people gathered on the cobblestone streets next to the canals. One could tell at a glance that they were residents rather than tourists, for they wore short-sleeved shirts, pressed jeans, and nice shoes.

Giorgio kicked a plastic bottle as he walked, dancing around it like a footballer. "So, then, I suppose you'd like a Morgana in your life. How about that actress?"

"Knock it off. Morgana is the ideal woman, the woman every man wants to love, and the woman every woman wants to be. But even though I am quite fond of her—perhaps I even love her—I would never write that stuff on the wall. Look!" He pointed at the graffiti on the wall of the old church: a large heart that read, *Mary, I love you forever.*

"Perhaps it's to the Virgin. Ever think of that?"

"I'm serious," Marco replied. "It's disgusting, the defacing of the old buildings. And I reiterate: even in love I would not do such a thing."

"You love your city and its bricks that much more, eh?"

Marco looked over and smiled. "I guess this is why I'm untakeable."

"Listen," said Giorgio, "not every man wants a woman who will enchant him into wrecking his ship on the rocks by just hearing the sound of her voice. As for you, since you are obviously in love with Morgana, no other woman can measure up. And *that* is why you don't have a girlfriend."

The two friends meandered through the *calle*s, eventually taking the route that passed through Saint Mark's Square. They walked along on the side of the *Mercerie* heading towards the *calle Mercerie Orologio.*

"Thank God, there's nobody here!" said Marco.

"I rarely come over here because it's so busy," said Giorgio, his voice so full of gratitude that it was almost dreamlike.

"It is nice when we can see Venice like it this and enjoy the old buildings, the sounds, and the smell of the city."

"Agreed."

"You know, every time I get to this point, I start holding my breath, as I want my next to be in St. Mark's Square."

"Where do you start holding your breath? Do you have some sign that will signal you to begin?"

"Indeed. As soon as I pass the *Calle Larga San Marco*, I hold my breath till I am under the Clock Tower, all ready to explode once I enter St. Mark's Square."

"And that helps?"

"It intensifies the enjoyment."

Giorgio erupted in laughter. "You are getting weirder by the month, Marco."

The man's laugh was contagious.

La piazza San Marco was breathtaking, with the majesty of the square on the right and the baroque church on the left. They walked just past the church and sat on the front step of the *Marciana Library*. As they stared up at the Doge Palace, water lapped gently against the gondolas tied to their posts for the night, resting in St. Mark's Basin.

"Valeri was right," said Giorgio, invoking the poet's name. "Venice is beautiful and strange at the same time."

"Look at you, referencing Valeri!"

"But it's true," Giorgio continued unabated. "The spired buildings standing out of the water, the *campielli* where people come together to celebrate life, the bridges. You need only look at this breathtaking cathedral to appreciate beautiful strangeness."

"You know, for all the trouble you give me, I'm glad you love our home as much I do."

"*Nobody* loves Venice as much as you do."

A cat jumped from behind an overflowing garbage can, startling the two men with a grating hiss.

It was an Egyptian Mau—Marco recognized the rare breed from the coat. One of his college professors had had a similar cat that he claimed was descended from the Sphinx.

Giorgio bent down and tried to coax the spitting beast with kissing sounds.

"Leave him alone, the poor thing," said Marco. "He probably doesn't want to listen to you go on about Valeri." He watched as the cat darted off toward the lagoon, passed through an archway, and disappeared into the darkness.

They continued walking, finally stopping at the library in front of two large granite columns bearing symbols of the two patron saints of Venice.

Marco admired the eastern column over its twin, with its winged lion perched atop, standing their chin up with the pride and patience of a sentry.

Bringing his gaze back toward Earth, he saw the unusual cat again. The Egyptian Mau had reappeared out of an alleyway on their right. "It's not only tourists who come from all over the world to visit Venice, but also the cats."

"Huh?"

Marco threw his jaw in the direction of the feline. "What do you think an Egyptian cat is doing in Venice?"

"Egyptian?"

"It's a Mau. From Egypt."

"Maybe he's on vacation?" Giorgio bent down again, this time with caution. The cat sat still on a piece of discarded cardboard and looked somberly at them. "I appreciate your love for our city, but you seem blind to anything that's wrong with it. The garbage, the constant smell of piss in the air." He continued as if self-conscious, explaining to the unexpected guest why everything was in such disarray. "You see, the canals haven't been cleaned for centuries. Italy has the technology to clean them, but the government won't do it because it costs money. Even efforts that cost nothing, like people picking up after themselves, are ignored. There is no motivation to care, and frankly, that confuses me." The look in the cat's eyes seemed to convey a parallel disgust.

"Come on," said Marco.

A shadow crept over Giorgio's face. His voice became leaden. "Everyone says they're proud to be Venetian, yet there is no pride in their actions." He shrugged. "Or lack of action, I guess." The cat's ears turned sideways.

"We haven't done enough either," said Marco. "There are few good men left who care. You hear that, Sphinxy? We bid you adieu and leave you to enjoy what's leave of our fine city."

They continued walking, their footsteps were airy. Marco stared down at his own hands, flexing them as if some magical power might be summoned to make everything all right. A gust of wind followed them, blowing food wrappers down the calle and bringing an acrid stench of piss into his nostrils.

Giorgio fell into step beside him. "God, have a whiff."

Marco shook his head. "I'm not blind. I know Venetian pride is mostly posturing and only government or university jobs are left. I've watched the port of *Marghera* shrinking as fewer businesses line its walkways and streets. Tourism has made it impossible for a Venetian to buy a home here. Even a one-bedroom apartment with a balcony cost more than a million Euros. For what? To look out onto the world's most ornate garbage scow. And yes, I've seen local people, people with jobs, squatting in broken-down old buildings and I watch the appalled rich tourists who come here. We've both seen them hauled out of those buildings against their will."

Giorgio rolled his eyes. "And don't get me started on *Marghera*, our favorite chemical time bomb."

"It's too late for *Marghera*," said Marco. "Let's leave it for another day."

"The night's over then?"

Marco smiled. "You haven't had enough commiserating for one night? Care to walk more and complain?"

The two men embraced. Giorgio headed back toward *Campo San Bartolomeo* and Marco struck out in the other direction, back to his family's home in *Campo Manin*. Marco glanced over his shoulder and saw his friend walking with one hand in his pocket, the other holding his shirt over his nose.

CHAPTER 5

TROUBLED WATER

Marco kept walking and was once again in La Piazza San Marco, alone. The Baroque cathedral was staring at him, stone portal arches raised in permanent, ancient query. The four bronze horses stood with ancient poise, each with one leg up mid-gait.

Marco squinted, and blinked. Yes. It was true. The horses were moving.

The legs had dropped, and the alternate legs raised. They continued like this, dropping raising, their heads nodding to the wind. Yet, they remained stationary. He felt as if he were staring through the slits of a zoetrope.

The Lion of Venice alighted between them on the apex of the arch.

A cold, choking sensation came over him. God had abandoned Venice.

There was a rush like blown thunder. Washed tumbled toward him, orange and yellow. Marco bent his knees, bracing himself against the oncoming wave.

And it was gone. He looked around. Everything was in its place. No lion atop the arch. Just a few pigeons. He realized he'd fallen to his knees.

He got up with a self-conscious gaze about him and started toward *Calle Della Mandorla,* where he'd eventually walk blindly to the house he lived in with his parents. On the way, he stopped and stood before the statue of Daniele Manin. Marco's home, the house he had grown up in, was located in *Campo Manin,* and had formerly belonged to the revered statesman after whom it was named. The statue had watched over that very house for generations. Marco looked up at the majestic monument in reverence as if he were in the presence of a pope or a king.

"Signor Manin," he said, for he often spoke to it as if it were his own personal guardian, "you have been watching over me since I was a child. Please help me understand what is going on. These are not mirages, right? Is there something I need to know? Am I going crazy?"

He paused, then, with a smile, added, "I am crazy, talking to a statue, yes?"

He stared at the base, the bronze pedestal made the figure seem even taller. A winged lion, the symbol of Venice, stared back at him. The now-familiar fear gripped his belly at the sight of it. It appeared to look directly across Rio de San Luca toward the house the leader had once lived in,. Despite the harsh patina of bronze, the leader's face appeared serene and decisive.

"Oh, Signore Manin," he said with a sigh, "I will do everything in my power to save our beautiful city. For you, I will do it."

It was a promise he had been making to this statue for as long as he could remember. And this time when he said it, a golden halo crowned Manin's head. The statue itself was shining, not reflecting light like usual, but producing its own light. He moved in closer, then broke the city ordinance and climbed upon the lion. He listened, for he swore he could detect a distant murmur emanating from with the statue as if a soul was trapped in an eternity of space and time inside it. He continued to watch the face of Manin. Not even a twitch.

And yet, he left the statue, glancing back at it more than once. Yes, the great man had heard his promise.

CHAPTER 6

THE LAST TRUE VENETIAN

Memories came to Marco of when he was a small boy. When he wasn't boisterously chasing pigeons, he was extolling the virtues of Venice to tourists. He especially enjoyed telling them of Daniele Manin, who defended the city from Austria in the name of Italian unification. Though none of his compatriots could imagine such a thing, it did happen, well after the great man's death.

Marco Bello's family lived in a home right inside the Campo Manin, one of the largest squares in Venice. When his father told him of the house's famous resident, the thought warmed the sensitive young man and subsequently added a flair of conceitedness to his tour guide spiel.

Every room in the house had a Venetian terrace, a particular floor common in the past consisting of one slab. Past the entrance was a large corridor; on the right was a kitchen with handsome marble cabinets. The kitchen is large enough to serve as a dining room as well. The large sitting room adjacent faced the campo where they could see the Manin statue. A doorway divided the day area from the three bedrooms and a bathroom. Although most of the bedrooms were in the back of the house facing the calles, Marco's bedroom window looked out onto the campo and the statue of Manin. Most of the furnishings in the house seemed old-fashioned to him, as his mother liked old furniture, paint with a weathered look, couches, and carpets that knew strange, heavy bodies of the past. Despite the house's status as a living specter of time, Marco's room was cozy. It had a large desk over which was displayed a small galleon in a glass. and Dali's paint "Mask of pain" hung on the wall.

As a child, he liked to sit for hours staring outside his window at the statue of Manin. He would imagine Manin fighting the Austrian hordes. But what captured Marco's imagination and heart most of all was the lion that stood at the foot of the statue, wings spread as if ready to take off. The lion was protecting his beloved city and he was glad for it.

It had been a very long night and Marco was mystically minded. He began to recall images from early childhood. His grandmother was one of the people who entered this zone. She had died six years before, but in his memory, she was taking Marco from the ward in which he was born to the neonatal intensive care unit of the hospital to have emergency surgery. He had been born in the old *San Giovanni e Paolo* hospital, which looked more like a church than a hospital in the *Castello district* of Venice.

His grandmother, Maria, appeared now before him and repeated what he had heard many times before.

"You are a miracle, baby."

"Why do you say that, Nonna?" he asked, as curiously as he did the first time she had told him.

She smiled. One of her teeth was black. "When it was time to bring you home from the hospital, your mother was too weak to walk, so your mother and your father took a boat to carry you home. As she was sitting in the back of the boat, a gust of wind hit the boat, and your mother dropped you, and you fell into the water."

"Yes, and then?"

"And one of the forked waves on either side of the engine rose high into the air and caught you. The wave crashed into the boat, soaking everyone, but it placed you right in the lap of your mother. You weren't even coughing. Your face must have never gone underwater. It was like the water itself bore you unto your mother like Moses."

"It sounds like a fairy tale," he said to the apparition.

Maria grinned widely, beautiful as she was in life. "Everybody thought your mother was crazy when she told us. She had seen a mirage or had some fantastic dream. But I am telling you, I believed her because when they reached home, their clothes and your blanket were all wet, as if you had just taken a shower or a bath. It was a nice, sunny day, too, so it couldn't have been raining."

"A mirage" he laughed, "like a Morgana mirage."

She nodded appreciatively. "I saw Morgana. She had a large green gown matching her eyes. Her hair moved freely in the air. She smiled at me and then disappeared. When I repeated this, everybody was telling me I was a crazy old woman, so I stopped talking about it. But I really saw her. Don't tell anyone that I told you or else they'll think I'm still crazy!"

"Well then, Nonna, it shall remain our secret."

His grandmother left him to the rest of his memories. With tears in his eyes, he recalled his early years playing in the Campos with his uncle Vittorio, stopping every so often to stare with wonder at the numerous statues. A dozen years older, Vittorio always encouraged Marco's curiosity and enjoyed telling him many stories about the city, for he loved her as well. Nonna and Vittorio had bequeathed their deep and abiding love for Venice to Marco.

Vittorio often took Marco on walks around the city, talking for hours at a time. Marco listened with rapt attention until he was able to tell stories of his own. From then on, he never missed the opportunity to improvise guided tours of Venice to any tourist that would pay him the least amount of interest. Within a couple of years, he earned a reputation for being a better guide and telling more entertaining stories than the professionals.

Most of the time, Marco was happy but lonely. And as he grew older, he began to wish for a companion other than Giorgio. For while his friend had a spirit that emanated from the same place as his own, he longed for someone does not like himself. He wanted to talk, to be understood. But he knew that love was really a melding of *strange* worlds. And he was also an idealist and pined for the unconditional love of starry romances.

He was twenty years old and had not yet had a serious relationship or experienced romantic love. Only God knew how much he had been yearning for it. And so, God gave him Venice.

None of his peers had seemed like worthy prospects. He loved good conversation, but most of his female friends seemed silly or even ignorant. Indeed, most of the girls he met or were introduced to appeared so detached from real life that he was astounded by their lack of depth. How could they spend so much of their time in activities whose only value was dictated by a society that worshipped superficial beauty, the rich, and the famous? If it were destined for him never to find true love, at least while he attended University, he would settle for simple companionship, escaping only to make love to Venice. Shallow, transient relationships could never compensate for the treasure of intellectual, emotional, and spiritual synergy.

For all his impossible standards, Marco was not at all unlikeable. His fellow students appreciated his empathetic demeanor and demonstrated by confiding in him. He was well-liked among the university professors as well, being respectful and diligent in his studies.

"Are you an only child?" DiCenzo, his first professor, had asked him one day.

Marco admitted that yes, he was the sole bearer of the family name.

"I would never have guessed. You have impeccable manners and a strong work ethic. Your self-discipline is admirable and rarely seen in students at this level. These traits will hold you in good standing wherever you go on campus or in business."

DiCenzo was southern, and good manners were the most important things to have in life.

So, if it wasn't the character lacking in Marco, what was it?

CHAPTER 7

POLLUTED WATER

The next morning, Marco awakened to the sirens sounding, indicating high tide. He looked out the window but there was no water in the calles. He took a quick coffee and went down to see what was going on. As he walked through *Calle Vallaresso* to Piazza San Marco, people were congregating along one of the adjacent canals. This was unusual, so he went over to see what the fuss was about. At the back of the crowd he tapped a young woman on the shoulder.

"What's going on?"

"Are you blind?" she said. "Have a look."

Marco's heart skipped a beat. The water was yellow and bubbling with gas.

"They have to close Marghera!" he said to her. "Enough with the chemical plant! They have to close it. We can't live this way."

He dialed Giorgio's number.

"This had better be good," his friend answered groggily. "I was dreaming of Monica Bellucci."

"I'm in Piazza San Marco. The water is yellow and bubbling."

Silence for a moment, then. "Another mirage?"

"No, other people see it, too! A huge crowd has gathered."

TV reporters began to amass. Locals and tourists were taking selfies with the dirty water.

Giorgio arrived out of breath and went pale when he saw the water.

"I didn't think it could be true," he said.

"We both had this vision," said Marco, who was beginning to break with fear.

"Major Ongaro just declared an emergency. He's alerting *Malcontenta* and *Mestre*."

People in the crowd started coughing from the toxic gas. Someone yelled, advising everyone to cover their faces. Marco heeded the suggestion. The odor penetrated his sleeve and his eyes began watering.

"I thought they were turning the Marghera into a green zone," he complained.

"Must be some corrupt people still producing the dangerous chemicals just to profit."

The chemical plant of Marghera was far away but close enough to affect all. A forest of chimneys belched smoke of different colors. Huge round tanks to store petrol and chemicals were competing with shipyards to dominate this devastatingly ugly industrial smudge on the flat landscape. Canals flowing into the lagoon were continually dumping chemical waste. It had now reached Venice, swirling out of the narrow channels into the shallow, weed-filled water of the lagoon and transforming it from its normal gray-brown.

Marco was asking himself questions about the real meaning of his dream the previous night in the theater, concluding that it wasn't an illusion but a premonition. He needed to do something, but he didn't know what; then he suddenly remembered something.

"Damn, what time is it? I'm late."

He started running despite the toxic air, covering his face with his shirt. Maybe he would have a chance to discuss the situation at the university, and get some answers.

CHAPTER 8

THE LECTURE ABOUT MANIN

He made it to class just on time. He would not miss this class for the world. It was about his hero, Manin. The professor was already in the room and at the podium, preparing his notes. Professor Grassi was Marco's favorite history teacher at the university. He was a good man who always supported the students; they loved his classes not only because it was clear he had an extensive depth of knowldge, but also because he was a good listener.

The lecture scheduled for that day was on the history of the Venetian Revolution. With a curly dark beard and thick glasses, Professor Grassi exuded an air of dignified competence. He began his lecture in a modulated voice: "In 1856, Manin met with Italian Prime Minister Cavour to talk about Italian Unification. Later, writing about the meeting, Cavour wrote that he and Manin discussed '*l'unità d'Italia ed altre corbellerie*' (the unity of Italy and other nonsense), thus signaling his preliminary prejudice against it. Though Manin died the following year, his writings were integral to the ultimate success of Italian Unification." The professor's voice rang clear and the words resonated with Marco. No subject could be more dear to him, for he revered Daniele Manin and hoped to become a man of his qualities one day.

"Manin was a true statesman," Professor Grassi continued." He was a man of vision with impeccable integrity. He had been declared the Lion of Venice for his leadership and courage during those difficult years when Venice was forced to resist multiple invasions. All true Venetians know that the lion at the foot of the statue of Manin is another representation of the man himself." The professor adjusted his glasses and looked up from the podium.

Despite his genuine wish to learn more about his hero, Marco could not help but be a little distracted, for he kept thinking about Venice's current situation with chemicals invading the lagoon. Unfortunately, it was just one of multiple plagues upon the city.

When class ended, Professor Grassi approached Marco. "Marco, how you are doing?" Marco assured him he was well, but the professor continued. "I have the impression you were mentally absent from the discussion today; I thought you liked the history of Manin." A look of worry crossed Marco's face; the professor asked, "You look so anxious. Are you truly okay?"

Professor Grassi had known Marco and his family for years. He remembered when Marco was in junior high school, and the young man was trying to be a tour guide. Marco's intimate knowledge of the background to his home and his love for it made him impassioned about the details; every time he explained them, visitors and onlookers alike were affected by his enthusiasm and became eager to learn more.

Marco unconsciously shook his head as he answered, "Did you see the toxic gas coming out of the water this morning?"

Moving to his desk, Grassi answered, "I heard the sirens and overheard some of the students mentioning it, but I didn't see it for myself."

Marco quickly explained the situation and his dream, at which point Grassi's mouth hung open, stunned.

"What do you think about my dream?"

"Marco, as a philosopher, I have a hard time accepting that it was premonition since I do not believe in supernatural phenomenon, but I trust your sincerity and your story is quite believable." Seeing the earnest look on his student's face, he added, "I really don't know what to think about it."

The two men thought in silence for a while, then Marco decided to change the subject. "Even so, I was engaged with your lecture, Professor, but I admit that I was also a bit distracted. I didn't realize how much the situation in Venice is affecting me emotionally..." Knowing that the professor was such a good listener always encouraged his students to confess things they usually did not share with others. "You know, I always wanted to be like Daniele Manin." Before Grassi could reply, Marco added, "I bet Manin would be terribly disappointed if he could see Venice today. I think we have new invaders now."

The professor screwed up his face in puzzlement.

Marco continued. "The invading hordes are no longer armies bent on conquering the territory of this beautiful city. They are tourists. And unlike those armies of old, they are aided by locals who have lost all hope because they have no other option than to think of the factories as the only way to earn an income." He paused, his face flush, ashamed of his quivering voice, then said, "The weapon of the modern barbarian is apathy."

Though silent for a moment, Professor Grassi considered the validity of Marco's righteous indignation. "I believe you are correct. We have different enemy, but they are just as dangerous. What's more, we allow them to do whatever they want in our city in the name of profit."

Having one's concerns truly heard has a way of calming the nerves. Marco took a cleansing breath. "Isn't our history full of these examples?"

Professor Grassi's mouth curled into a smirk. "I'm afraid it's the history of humanity, my friend."

CHAPTER 9

THE SAVIOR OF VENICE

"So, what can we do about it?" Marco was beginning to feel hope now that someone seemed to share his perspective. "It seems that nobody cares anymore."

"I have to agree with you again," replied Professor Grassi. "No one has a handle on what to do. There is no plan to regulate the flux of tourists or educate the Venetians on how best to clean up our town, and I can go on and on. I am a professor of history, and it's frustrating to admit that it seems our history has not taught anything to anyone. As the cliche goes, history is repeating itself. Venice's demise is just around the corner. Indeed, it is upon us."

They looked at each other gravely.

"You know," Grassi continued after a moment, "some people called you the Savior of Venice after your letter to the newspaper, not to mention that essay you wrote."

Marco recalled the open letter he penned to the mayor and sent it to the local newspaper, *La Nuova Venezia* while he was in his second year. In it he had expressed his concern for the deterioration of the city. He now remembered the feeling of compulsion to write that missive, as it was in a moment of feverish intensity. He followed the letter with an essay titled, "The Death of the Lady", which won the Proud of Venice award.

Professor Grassi smiled. "Others suggested you might be the new paladin of Venice. Did you know that? The letter made such an impression on people because it was clear it was written with heart and soul. You even went to visit the mayor at City Hall. You were a senior in high school, no?"

"I was a sophomore. We gathered at City Hall. The mayor met me and shook my hand in front of the news photographers. After that, he hardly had two words to spare for me." Marco's voice hardened as he recounted the tale. "He effectively told the children that everything will be fixed, everything will be perfect. He praised the children as the generation which will bring the fair city of Venice back to her glory. It was a bullshit speech. Like most politicians, he knew how to speak well and make promises in front of a crowd."

The professor put a hand on his shoulder. "Marco, it may be difficult to picture it, but I once was young and hopeful. It was only after I achieved tenure that I realized I had become jaded and cynical. You have not earned that right, yet."

Marco began to interject and Grassi stayed him.

"I still remember when I spoke to you after graduation. You were complaining that the mayor had no vision. Rightly so. But you know that we have a new one now, and he seems better than the last one."

Marco went silent as he remembered that time when he had felt more alone than ever before in his young life. After all of the attention from the letter had died down and it became clear the mayor was not going to make any of the promised changes, Marco became somewhat of a joke among his friends. Some of them had indeed accused him of being a paladin. At times Marco had felt like his world was sinking like Venice and would eventually drown. He hadn't been surprised to learn from a study by the Scripps Institution of Oceanography that Venice was sinking one to two millimeters a year. Worse, he began to realize that it would not be the last time that he would be let down. His disappointment and frustration were so overwhelming, it was tempting to live as if there were no hope. But he was not like those Venetians who had given up, choosing to live in filth, or who had already moved to the mother land.

His hope had not yet died after all. Something within him refused to give up. His determination sometimes waned but his pure love for the city remained. It was more than admiration for her classic beauty. Something in her spirit captivated him. Could environmental awareness empowered by passion translate into savviness capable of bringing about true, enduring change?

"What is going through your head?" said the professor.

"Uncertainty about the future."

"Ah," said Grassi, a wry smile on his face, "you think about the future after all! Listen to me, I teach history because the past can teach us a lot. But you mustn't be sad for it. You must enjoy the present and work in hope for the future, and that's it. I know you will do something good for our community. I feel it. Marco, why don't you write an open letter to the newspapers, addressing in detail once more the problems of Venice? I bet they will publish it."

Marco stepped toward the desk to give his professor a firm handshake. "Thank you, Professor; I will do it and I am going to try my best."

He went straight to the library, wrote the letter, and emailed it to the local paper. On his way home, he stopped in Campo San Toma. He was tired and did not want to walk to get to the other side of the canal, so he took a gondola to cross. This wasn't an ordinary gondola. It was the most secret gondola in the labyrinth of Venice, its location known only to residents. As he crossed the canal, he saw the Rialto Bridge. Thank God and Danielle Manin, it was still there.

CHAPTER 10

ENVIROMENTAL ABUSE

Marco's mother had come from a railroader family, as had her husband. Each of their families had been in charge of a railroad station near Venice. Giovanni had met Rosa in school and was immediately taken by her, insisting against her protests that she resembled a young Sofia Loren. Now that she was older, she still had gentle features and had kept her shape. She rejected the term "aging gracefully", preferring instead to educate the utterer of that abominable phrase that this was indeed how women aged, and that it was ungracefulness that was aberrant.

As a young woman, Rosa had loved her job as an elementary school teacher and she loved raising her only child, her son. Marco was a delight. From time to time, though, she expressed worry to her husband that the boy never spoke about or brought home a young woman for them to meet. After all, he was twenty-one. But in her old-fashioned way, she was too reserved to ask him. Instead, she felt that children needed to find their own way in life.

At dinner, Marco's father uncorked a locally produced Sauvignon Blanc to go with the tortellini and pesto. Giovanni was about Marco's height and still had all his hair. He had a young face, with pronounced cheekbones and the aquiline nose of a Teutonic statesman. His gentle manners mirrored his ancient and tired soul. His spirit had been scarred by a difficult upbringing. After the second world war, he had lost first his father and then his mother—all before he had reached his teens. Giovanni put himself through school, wanting to be a doctor, but settled for a degree in chemistry, claiming the discipline to be "more precise". Trained in public health, he worked as a pharmaceutical expert with the Health Commission of the city of Venice. A proclivity for athletics had made him suppress an intolerance for weakness, and he could be commanding and overbearing, but his personal sensibilities were kind and caring and showed in his more vulnerable moments. Indeed, his gentle demeanor seemed constantly at war with his nature as a scrapper, which often made him intolerable to others, including his only son. However, he was never malevolent and cared deeply about other people, even if he was a bit stubborn.

It is a pity life has not always been kind to him, Marco thought.

As he and his father sipped at their glasses, Rosa talked about the new art show coming to the *Museum Correr*. His family loved the Impressionists.

When his mother left the room, Marco asked, "Papa, did you see the yellow-orange water this morning?"

"I did not. But I smelled it in the air. Putrid."

"What's the Health Commission saying about it?"

"The usual. We've been trying to fix Marghera for years now, but are fighting an uphill battle. We have been trying to fight the system, but the system is fighting back, and you know the Italian bureaucracy. It could take decades to fix anything, even if it is a life-and-death situation like this."

"Papa, you can't just accept this. What is going on with the chemical pole in Marghera? I thought they were turning into a clean energy industrial pole?"

"The problem is that so many are against the changes by sheer dint of them being technological solutions to a natural problem."

"Is that rational?"

"No, but it's human."

"So, how do we fix it?"

"For one thing," his father said, filling his glass quickly and slowing the pour as it reached the rim, "we need to fight for a balance between industry and naturalism if you will."

"Okay, this is all good but you are talking like a politician now."

"Nonsense," said the man, waving off his son with a flair of arrogance. "Live a while longer and learn what life is like. Every time you go after the chemical companies, they come out with a study showing that nothing is wrong."

"Meanwhile, the lagoon gets more and more polluted. It's a giant, dirty puddle."

"Okay, yes, and if the chemicals are not extracted from the water, it spreads easily and is then very difficult to clean. You're boring me with truisms."

"What do the local authorities say?"

His father straightened up, affecting the plastic posture of a public relations spin master. "This for immediate release: Pollution in the lagoon presents absolutely no health hazard for people living and working in the area."

"How can that be possible?"

"Why, don't you know, boy?" said his father, obviously succumbing to the effects of the good wine. "The last deputy mayor blamed it on the policies of the Socialists. Then Socialists blamed Christian Democrats. They blamed it on... oh, loose morals. And it was like playing jojo, on and on, without anybody really doing anything about the city. Oh, and added to this was an open inquiry suggesting that politicians were in bed with the chemical companies, leaving them free to pollute the lagoon with impunity. The pigs' shit in our water, if I may put it intellectually."

"Papa, we all need to stop blaming everyone else. Should everyone go to jail and only a few good men rebuild the city?"

Giovanni laughed, and there was the arrogant wave of the hand again. "You cannot accuse anyone. Besides, you know a trial in Italy takes anywhere from fifteen to a thousand years. My son, the optimist! A chemical company was once ordered to pay sixty-three billion lire and that's what? Something like ten billion euros? Paid in compensation to the families of a hundred and fifty petrochemical workers who had died of tumors after working in their factories. How can we rejoice have such wise men who know the true value of human suffering? Be sure and write them a letter, Marco. You're wonderful with words! Perhaps they'll even print it in the newspaper." The man convulsed in a fit of laughter.

Marco tightened his jaw. "Where is the vision for the future?"

His father composed himself. "Come again?"

"What is to become of my generation? We can't live in a country like this."

Giovanni's face went grave. "I saw many things in my life, including the last war. I still remember running with my brothers to the bomb shelter when airplanes were shitting bombs on our land. At least then you knew your enemies. Now you don't even know who is the friend and who is the foe. The only ones we can really trust are the rats. They know what benefits them. But do not fret, boy. Unless you live in a putrid house, they won't attack you." Giovanni chuckled shallowly. "Unfortunately, we don't have the funding to effectively rid the city of the pests. The rats in Venice seem to be quite resistant to our attempts at disinfestation." He had trouble with this last word, pronouncing and re-pronouncing it several times.

"Have you ever had one in your house, maybe when you grew up?"

"You want to hear a story? One day I came back home—this was before I met your mother—and I found a small, round hole in one of the kitchen windows screens. When the pest control operator visited the premises, he told me Venice was overrun with rats. He said that the island's sewer system was filled with them."

"I hate the sound of that."

His father looked at him with a sardonic expression. "No one likes rats, boy. Not even other rats."

"No," said Marco. "I hate that you're okay with it."

"I'm not okay with it and you can put your pity in a trunk somewhere."

"Papa, I didn't mean—"

"Oh, do not presume to reason with a drunken man." Giovanni's pleasant smile dispelled most of the tension in the conversation. "You know I love you."

"And I love you, Papa. Will you try harder?"

"The revolutionary polemicist is asking the civil servant to try harder! Yes, o sage of the people, yes, I will try harder!" Again, he broke down in a sloppy fit of laughter.

As it was by this time, well into the evening, Marco leaned over and kissed his father on the cheek. The stubble was rough and warm. And they retired for bed.

While they slept, dark clouds both above and below Venice invaded her, undetected, and stalked the calles and canals stealthily. They enveloped the city and penetrated her psyche like a nightmare, incrementally building strength, waiting patiently for just the right moment to ravage its prey.

A shiver scurried up Marco's backbone in his troubled sleep.

CHAPTER 11

THE FLYING DUTCHMAN

Awakened in a jolt, Marco reached for the nightstand and turned on the lamp, his heart racing. In this state, he recalled the words of Longfellow:

> *It is gone, and I wonder and wait*
> *For the vision to reappear.*

The echo of these words from Fata Morgana soothed him, and drifting back into sleep, he found himself on an ancient ship. The wood was freshly hewn and threw off their scents of tar into the salty wind. He was standing at the portside railing looking out onto the horizon where the sky met the flat gray ocean, and were white clouds descended, restrained in their oppression.

When he heard footsteps, he turned to see the ship's captain walking toward him, hand outstretched in greeting. The man wore a coat of purple, with ruffles tumbling out of the wrists and neck like sea foam. His hair was an immense tangle of wool that fell over his shoulders in a bush of chestnut brown.

"Captain Willem van der Decken, at your service. Welcome aboard the Flying Dutchman."

Marco shook the man's hand, noting that it was remarkably dry and stiff.

The captain laughed heartily. "If you could see your expression, lad. You don't know if you're dreaming or not. I assure you, you're dreaming. It is always my great honor to welcome someone who travels to us by dream. Those people have grand destinies. I'm glad to offer them what I can."

He walked toward the captain's bridge to check his compass.

"Offer?" asked Marco. "What use is it to give someone something in a dream only for him to lose it when he awakes? What could you possibly offer me?"

"Why, information, of course!" He frowned at his compass. "Damn compass never works when you need it to." He glanced back up at Marco. "I've had information piling up for you since the day you were born. You've been on quite a journey. A blind journey, since you were unaware of what was expected of you." He gestured toward the horizon. "We each have a blind journey set out for us. Most humans know this when they are born, but they do not know where they are to go. Who sets up our journey? Is everything written in the skies for us?" He frowned at the sky and shrugged his shoulders. "I do not know. I am a ghost, but I was once a captain. I was once someone, wasn't I? Was I always a ghost? Could it be I was born as a ghost? Might we all be ghosts?" He laughed, a rattling sound like rocks rolling around in a tin can. "The bad thing about being a ghost is that you have all of eternity to think inane thoughts."

The captain's eyes glittered. As he came towards Marco, a yellow and green parrot flew from the main canvas down to the helm. "Your destiny is to see us, to talk to us, to get a glimpse of a picture you never knew. You will see. Trust me."

The captain stretched out his hand and brought it uncomfortably close to Marco. This time Marco was reticent to touch it.

The man withdrew the hand self-consciously. "Huh. Give it time, and everything will be clear. I do not know much. In the end, I am just the captain of a ghost vessel that has been sailing forever. Payment for my hubris. You and I of the same stock. I was renowned for my speed and was rumored to be in league with the Devil." His face screwed up in mockery and the rattling laugh came again. "The Devil should know such company!"

"Then," said Marco, who was beginning to become very distressed and a little seasick, "why do you roam?"

"Ah, yes, well, hubris—that is the word for it. I thought I could weather the storm heading into Table Bay. I cursed the wind. I would see Table Bay or be damned, I said. I would reach the Cape of Good Hope if it took me to the Day of Judgement to do so. Well..." He tapped at the compass face. "It seems I must have been quite fervrent in my pronouncements. But, now that you are here, may you join me in feeling the souls of the lost. We appear to them, you know. Bad weather and loneliness bring us 'round."

"I don't want to join you," said Marco.

"Ah, but you have already." He turned his face toward the sea. "See that ship coming toward us?"

There was indeed a ship coming veiled and shimmering through the mist. As Marco watched, the ship silently approached the Flying Dutchman. The crew peered out in awe and wonder. A shiver ran down Marco's back.

The captain of the other ship called out to his crew. The voice was flat over the water. "That's not the *Flying Dutchman*! It's a Morgana mirage, a mere trick of light and air. Just watch. In a moment, I will prove it to you." He commanded one of his crewmen to climb up to the crow's nest. Once the crewman was up on high, he called down that there was another—very real—ship sailing just over their view of the horizon.

"See?" the captain called out. "A reflection in the water. Return to your posts or be lashed!"

"Had you been in that crow's nest," Captain van der Decken said, "you'd know that the poor slob had no choice but to lie to the captain. He's terrified right now because he saw nothing over the horizon. No ship but the fading mast of the Dutchman. And the crew knows it. I expect there will be some hushed talk among the men over the rest of the journey about what they saw. Each and every one of them believes he just had a brush with the Devil himself."

"But why does their Captain want to pretend he didn't see it, too?" Marco asked.

"Because fear is a shared secret, and one a captain would never divulge even were his life to depend upon it. But is that the lesson you learned?"

Marco shook his head.

"I thought so. Look at me. Look deeply. I thought to challenge God and the Devil. And now I pay for it. The storms that await you are not merely atmospheric occurrences. They are machinations that are there to prevent you from ascending to divine status. Heed them, or become as I am, dead and calling out to God with only the sorrow of loneliness as my answer."

A gale stirred and nearly knocked Marco off his feet. Soon he became aware of another sound—that of a woman singing. It came over him like a balm. He thought of Beatrice leading Dante out of Hell and cleansing his face of the stains. How sweet her touch much have been. He recognized then that these were the voices of Sirens. The chorus grew to a frenzied swirl of luscious melody, both a whisper and a roar. Frozen by it, Marco watched Captain van der Decken become a wisp, then a shade, and finally, misty air without a shape. With him, faded the Siren's song.

No, not faded... transmuted. For it had transformed into the tender voice of a woman, eerily beautiful.

"*Marco,*" the voice called out to him. "*Marco, continue to believe in me and our beloved Republic of Serenity, Venice. Marco, you are my final champion.*"

He startled himself awake with her words echoing in his mind, growing more and more distant.

He began to miss her terribly, tears streaming down his sweaty face. *I am in love with Morgana,* he thought. *Dear God.*

His desire became intense, for he suddenly realized that her voice had sounded so familiar. Where had he heard it before? His memory flashed back to a time before time. He remembered being rocked gently, then all of a sudden, he saw himself falling out of the hands of his mother, out of the boat and he was surrounded by water sloshing around him. He heard sounds, then a single sound—in a heartbeat rhythm—and he was back in his mother's arms. That was it!

That was where I heard your voice. Now I know I have met you before, even before this life. It was you, Morgana, who saved me from the water.

"*Marco, I am here at your side forever...*"

The voice grew ever more distant. Marco leaped up out of bed, then cried out as he realized he had landed on the floor.

No, please, dear Father in Heaven...

The vision was gone. And he waited in vain for it to reappear.

CHAPTER 12

LOSS OF ENCHANTMENT

He could not shake the cold feeling in his body. He tried drinking hot milk and hot coffee, but nothing warmed him. It was nearly summer and balmy outside, but he still needed a sweater as he walked outside and down the calle toward his favorite café. Even the extra layer of wool brought him no relief. Maybe it was the dream that had gotten under his skin. He realized that the cold was coming from inside of him.

In Rosa Salva Café in Campo San Luca he ordered another coffee. Since he was there, he decided to have breakfast and ordered a croissant. He picked up the *Il Gazzettino* from a table and sat nearby, at the stands. On the front page, was Marco's letter to the editor. The coffee came, steaming, and he let it cool a moment as he read his own words:

"Aristotle was correct in the Art of Rhetoric when he said, 'The citizenry can talk a lot and never accomplish anything.'"

"The city of Venice, at one time the crown jewel of the Adriatic Sea and home of the most exquisite glass, a haven for artists and their patrons to isolate themselves from a cruel and decadent world, is now a shadow of its former self." He glanced around, wondering if anyone else in the café was reading the same article. A few read newspapers, heads down, engrossed.

"It is impossible to walk the calles without the stench of urine permeating your nostrils. Trash and litter blow around the canals like leaves in late autumn. The canals are beyond filthy. The only people who swim in them now have a death wish, as they are worse than wallowing in a septic tank. For all of my life, I have fought to get Venetians to change their behavior, to find some pride in themselves, and to start caring for our city once again. Many talk a good game. None have lived it so far. In the last few days we witnessed an environmental disaster with our water turning yellow, and we breathe acid air. And yet nobody has been saying more than a few words in the papers. I hear Venetians say that we are the proudest city, filled with the most conscientious people. But when I walk her calles, it is clear that we are a city in denial of our laziness and hubris." He picked up the coffee, blew on it to cool it faster, and took a sip.

"I am proud to say I am a Venetian. I am ashamed to admit most Venetians litter without a thought." He looked up again, contemplating, then he took another sip of his coffee and read more. "How difficult is it to take the wrapper from a piece of candy and toss it into a trash can? What about pieces of paper, drink cups, food containers? The chemical company needs to clean the water and the air before is too late but a little cleaning up by everyone will also help us all."

He was thinking about how he could have added more, about how men urinate in the canals and on walls, apparently oblivious to the stench. They talk as if they are important men, but no matter their title, they probably only return to some menial job they are ashamed of. One time he saw the postman stop in one campo and urinate, then as if nothing happened, he had continued to deliver the mail. Disgusting.

Marco did not want to think about all the pets who were relieving themselves on the streets with few owners cleaning up after them. The people must have grown too lazy, tired, or jaded. Look at his father. The man had to deal with people every day who complained or talked well but did not want to do anything to improve the environmental situation of Venice themselves. They did not even care enough to bother changing anything, nor did they get involved in local politics or civic concerns. Just picking up their trash would be a start!

Marco's letter ended with a passionate plea: "You may not believe me, but our city is dying, and we will witness it in my lifetime if our current behavior remains the norm. I love our home. Don't you? I beg each of you to take pride in yourselves, in our city, and in our ability to turn things around and finally take care of her."

He had signed the lengthy letter simply, as before, with just his name: Marco.

In the café, people were asking him about the letter and complimented him on it. He humbly accepted their comments but inwardly wished they would take them to heart. In fact, some were jealous. One young guy in particular eating a pastry with his cappuccino bragged to his companion that he could have written a better letter. He overheard an old woman caked with unflattering makeup complain to the woman beside her.

"His musings on Venice are as murky as his knowledge of Aristotle."

Finally, two old men huffed and grumbled "What does he know about chemical waste? He's just a kid, and he should keep his mouth shut. Who does he think he is?"

Marco left the cafe disgusted. He knew they were trying to get under his skin.

He heard similar comments on a daily basis over the course of the next few weeks at the university, mostly from students but also from some faculty members. He felt terribly alone again, only cheering up when Giorgio and he talked. As time passed, he wondered more and more why people did not see what he could see, and why the ones who could were so indifferent. He continually felt down and hurt but he chose not to show it.

For good or bad his letter was shared on the web and became a popular topic of conversation. One day, tired of it all, he decided to go home for lunch in between classes. A letter awaited him in the mailbox.

To: Signor Marco

From: The Office of the mayor of Venice

The Mayor would be grateful for the pleasure of your company in his office to discuss possible solutions to our environmental issues. Please call to arrange a visit at your earliest convenience.

With regards,

Massimo Ongaro

The new Mayor—rather than his secretary—had signed the letter.

"Oh, no!" thought Marco. "Another mayor, another political game?" Will this mayor use him as a pawn and drop him like the other did? Perhaps not. But then, all politicians were the same at heart. He expected them all to have the same callous attitude. Surely he would be brushed off again. Or used for campaign candy like before. But his Papa had said that this mayor was different. Back and forth he argued with himself, wondering whether the letter was a precursor to trouble or a sincere effort to enlist his help. Would he be taken seriously, after all? Would something get done to save the city?

That Friday, Marco went to Ca' Loredan, the city hall, to meet with the mayor. Sitting in the spacious waiting room, he tried not to tap the floor with nervous feet, but failed. It was Venetian terrace, a mix of marble and cement, and every click echoed. He recalled the disappointment he had felt there many years before, when the previous Mayor had invited him to his speech to assuage the frustrations of the citizens by promising everything and doping nothing. Mayor Ongaro's office looked onto the Canal Grande and the Rialto Bridge. Marco looked at the paintings and an old tapestry on the sturdy hardwood walls, which soothed him to no end. One of them was from Canaletto.

He tapped his foot in time with the passing seconds. The room smelled of old paint, but it was clean enough. The open window whisked ghosts of stuffy conversation out into the passing breeze. From the open window came sounds of people walking on the calles below and voices talking on the boats passing by on the Grand Canal, the very place that had been in his dream.

The mayor must have forgotten his appointment. Marco picked up a local newspaper from the stack on the end table and flipped through the pages, landing on an article titled, "The Religious Gangs." Disruptive gangs in Venice, only two nights before, had broken into a violent fight over religious preference. Marco found himself not even paying attention to what religion they were but was horrified that they were fighting about religion at all in Venice. This was an abomination. Wasn't Venice one of the most tolerant cities he had ever known? He held that thought because from the corridor came the sound of heavy, hurried footsteps.

The secretary announced that the mayor was ready to receive him. Massimo Ongaro had a good reputation for getting things done, at least. Marco decided that he would give him a chance. Marco entered the room with guarded hope.

"Marco? Pleased to meet you." The mayor got up from his desk to shake the young man's hand. "I have read your article. My staff pointed it out to me. They know you, apparently. Or at least have heard of you."

He gestured for Marco to sit. "Your love of Venice rivals my own. It may well be greater than mine, though if it is, I have work to do." He smiled.

He was a tall, soft-spoken man. Apparently in good shape, but he looked a bit older than fifty-eight, and older than the picture Marco had seen in newspapers and on the internet, for his long beard and mustache were the color of spent coal.

The man's dark eyes assessed Marco all the while he spoke. Maybe that piercing look was due to the mayor's great wisdom. Marco had heard he was a learned man. What he knew about this man was limited, but... strange. The mayor was darting his eyes about the room. He seemed to look for something in the room. Perhaps something to show Marco.

As they began to talk, Marco, still standing, learned the mayor had been a professor of Philosophy in Venice, and then he had gone to Milan. His family, though, was from Venice, and he had lived in San Toma. The mayor had returned to Venice in order to help the town. Though he was not a professional politician, his demeanor and his knowledge were so impressive that the other candidate proved to be weak competition. Beyond exceptional intelligence, the mayor had high moral standards and was honest. That was unique, considering he worked in the corrupt Italian political system.

The mayor sat down at his desk and motioned once more for Marco to take a seat across from him. "I have always had a weakness for a sharp fellow with a sense of social responsibility and civic duty," he began.

"Your mission is noble and good, and I am sorry to say more necessary than even you may know. You are not a politician. However, I can see that you are a leader. The people have paid attention to what you have written, even when they do nothing. I have actually been reading your letters and articles in the newspaper since that first one you wrote as a young boy. Your purpose is clear and unwavering. Venice needs you. I need you. Might you consider working with me?"

For a moment, Marco just sat there, stunned. Not many had ever seemed to understand his vision before. Certainly not someone who had significant power. This man, at least from what he said, had been following Marco's work from the beginning and he seemed to get it.

"Marco, we have a great opportunity to raise awareness about our great city's peril. Would you be willing to come give a talk to the City Hall Open Forum this Sunday? I can get you in as one of the speakers."

"I'd be honored, Sir," Marco stated simply.

"Excellent!" the mayor exclaimed, clapping his hands like a delighted child. "To show that I mean what I say, I would like to meet you at the cafe in Campo San Luca. You know the one. It has been there since well before you were born. I would like to arrange weekly meetings with you there, say Friday mornings, beginning next week. Would that work for you? I wish I could promise you that we'll save Venice, but I can only promise that we'll try."

As Marco left the mayor's office for the first time since he had begun his quest, he felt a small but certain glimmer of hope.

CHAPTER 13

THE BOOK WITH THE MYSTERIOUS SCENT OF A WOMAN

Marco walked toward Saint Helena, at the tip of Venice facing the Lido and the open lagoon, just after the Arsenale, where the Venetians built boats and gondolas. It was a lovely garden space with parks, greens, and a soccer field. Marco was still reflecting about what he and Giorgio had last talked about.

He often went to Saint Helena when he was frustrated because he could practice the long jump in the athletic area around the soccer stadium. Not many tourists visited the park but many residents jogged there. Mothers took their children to see trees, lawns, and little squirrels. It was one of the few places in Venice where one could find both serenity *and* clean air.

Marco regularly did the long jump like a form of training. It both exhausted and exhilarated him. All forms of exercise brought him joy, but the marks he left in the box of sand during the long jump gave him an opportunity to measure his progress. With each jump, Marco could see whether or not he had improved from the last time. He could tell if his training was moving him in the right direction. He wished he could measure similar progress in his efforts to save Venice. He sometimes imagined himself doing the long jump across the Grand Canal or even across the Venetian Lagoon onto Lido. While he was suspended in midair, at times, he imagined he could see the land beneath him become magically free of all litter, stench, and vermin, returning to its pristine, classical beauty. He could see at the tides of decadence recede, never again threatening Venice's shores.

Perhaps if someone could build a real door from the bottom of the lagoon as an entrance or a gateway, to open and close according to the sea conditions, that would help. Maybe without the high tide, they could clean the bottom of the canals and remove the silt threatening the buildings, and strengthen their structures to last for another ten thousand years or more. Maybe the people would be happier and care more for their city and for each other. Who knows? Was this thought also merely a dream?

After a rigorous workout of long jumps at Saint Helena, Marco decided to break his pattern and take the touristy route home. He needed to surround himself with people to clear his head. Here, the breeze coming from the lagoon smelled like an open sea. The salty, soft smell from the water and the sweet scent of flowers growing in the park invited Marco to sit and enjoy the day. A little squirrel scurried up a tree when Marco approached. Marco sat on a bench where he could feel the soft wind coming from the sea. The lagoon reflected the sunlight, and all the boats passing by had twins: shadows running parallel on the clear water. It was one of the few times he had actually seen such shadows. It is hard to see a shadow sitting on a dark surface, when the water is not clear. Unfortunately, the water in the canals was not very clear.

It was still light out. Marco decided to make a stop in St. Mark's square. Just opposite the Cathedral, he noticed that the Impressionist painting exhibition had opened at the Museo Correr. Ever since Marco was a child, he had loved those paintings where colors and figures were mixed. At times, he could not even recognize a figure there, but it did not matter because he would always be moved by their game of colors. Like a video game in which you run after a villain, Marco chased each color on the canvas. The pursuit filled his heart with joy.

Marco decided to stop in. He entered the building and walked upstairs using the old marble steps, spacious enough to fit five people per step but now half closed for restoration.

The original walls of the old building were well-kept, in their original color. At the top of the stairs were glass doors. Using his student discount, he bought a ticket for the show. Right in front of him upon the huge wall hung the first example of pointillism. In the exhibit hall, Marco sat on a wooden bench for a good half hour in front of Van Gogh's *Starry Night*. Both versions of the painting were on display side-by-side: the older one, more structured. And the newer one, with the definition of the stars not as traditionally depicted, where Van Gogh's powerful use of color created a feeling that, for Marco, transcended any classical rules of painting. "Van Gogh was a genius," Marco thought to himself. Marco remembered when he had read about the artist's personal life, how no one would buy his work, how he was poor and supported by money his family sent him, his depression, his unrequited love, and ultimately his suicide. "He suffered a lot," Marco thought. "He must have expressed that suffering through his painting."

As Marco meandered toward another exhibit room, he noticed a little book on the floor beneath a bench. He picked it up. Electric shivers ran through his body, and he dropped the book on the floor. Then the shivering left. He leaned down to pick up the book again and he quivered, butterflies in his stomach, and hesitated for a moment. There was something strange about this book. It was well-worn. He picked it up and turned it over. Emblazoned on the cover was the title, *La Vita Nova*, (The New Life) by Dante, the father of the Italian language. Every Italian reads Dante in high school as he is considered "*Il sommo poeta*," the greatest poet of all. He remembered reading this book during his sophomore year. Marco held the famous story of unrequited love, warming his hands against the binding.

He brought the book close to his face. He could smell a scent like a woman's perfume. He sniffed again. It was Fendi, a sensual perfume. He looked around. No one else was in the room. He wondered whom it belonged to. He opened the book and flipped through the first few yellowed pages. There were scribbles inside, but he could find no name or address of the owner. Looking closer at the notes, he could not figure out what language they were. They were definitely not Italian. They were in different colors—green, purple, and orange, and seemed to be written in the same order, as if in some kind of sequence. He flipped through more pages. Green, purple, orange, again and again. He recognized repeating sequences of characters, but what language was it? What did the notes say? Marco looked around again. The room was still empty. Was this the volume of a student from his university? Clear,ly it was the work of a learned hand. Who else would annotate a book of poetry?

He became intrigued by how the changes of color were defined. There was almost a rhythm to the markings. Something he could not quite explain, yet it drew his attention. Finally, after scanning the interior once more, he could connect with one word, maybe the most important aspect. There was an orange circle around "Love" and an arrow to the margin with the word *Liefde*. What was that? Might it mean love? But in what language?

Marco was so lost in this book that he did not realize that the museum was about to close and he would be the last one inside. As he passed them, he saw that all the offices had closed early. He had already decided he must take the book with him all the better.

Marco went straight to the internet café. He logged onto one of the public computers and entered the word "Liefde." To his surprise it means: Love, Amore, Amour, all of them were there! It means love in Dutch. Yes, love. But this could not be just any type of love. Did the word Liefde refer to someone in particular or something? Can it be a supernatural love? A love that goes beyond all genders and walls of fear? For him to find a book like this, and not find the owner of that word…

He was bound to look for her. For it was a woman's hand. He was sure of it.

Marco went home where his mother had prepared risotto with shrimp and a salad for supper. As he sat at the table with his parents, his father asked, "So, Marco, you've been out all day. What were you doing?"

"I went running at Saint Helena and took a long walk home."

Marco had completely forgotten about the Impressionists, even though he knew how much his parents loved them, but he was so enthralled by his discovery of the book and that alien word *liefde*, that his mind was somewhere else.

His parents ate, talking about the food, how fresh the shrimp tasted, and about how the simple flavors of the risotto allowed them to appreciate the flavor of the shrimp itself. Marco, however, said nothing, for he could not get his mind off of the book. When he had finished eating, he kissed his parents good night and went to his room. He lay on his bed pondering the book. Who could have lost it? Whoever it was must have been a highly literary, sensitive being to have been reading Dante.

"I hope she is a young intelligent woman," Marco said to himself. "She must be intelligent, because she can write in more languages than just one."

His imagination ran wild. "What if it is Morgana herself giving me a clue. Maybe this is how she has decided to come and visit me. Oh, Morgana, if only you were here."

And if it is not Morgana? "Please, God, make her a nice, intelligent, sensitive girl. What if she is not Italian? Well, I guess for the first time I will love a tourist!"

"Maybe I can find her." He rolled over and hugged the book. She would become his sweet, secret love. With these thoughts dancing in his head, Marco fell asleep holding the book in his hands. Soon he recognized a familiar, sweet voice coming to him in a dream.

"I love you, Marco, *liefde*.... My *liefde*." The identity of the woman was still a mystery. Marco found himself in a strange house with multiple floor and stairs. The woman was running towards the second and then towards the third floor and Marco was chasing after her.

"Wait, wait for me." They were in a long corridor and she was always out of reach.

"Liefde, my liefde," the woman said again.

"Please stop! Come back." He was running upstairs again but felt the stairs were vertical and he had to fight gravity. One stair after another one, first going up then right, then left, then up again. She was there, her image reflecting in every direction, like in a glass house, as if the stairs had mirrors.

"Wait, please wait! Talk to me!" The stairs were almost moving.

He had almost reached her when a flood of water rose from the bottom of the house to stop him from following her.

As he battled the water, trying to breathe, he emerged in Piazza San Marco, crowded as usual. He glimpsed her, recognized her hair, but he could not pick his way through the crowd and she melted into it.

"Wait, wait," but the noise of the crowd drowned his voice.

"I love you, too. Don't leave me. Please, come to me."

He suddenly woke up. The book was still in his right hand. *La Vita Nova*, a new life, maybe this was the starting of a new beginning for him, as well. A new perspective, a new love.

He had received the intimation, unbidden, that when dreams are truly desired, they can become a reality.

PART II

CHAPTER 14

A SECRET WORLD

Daniele Manin woke up hoping, yet again, that he had been dreaming. Unlike all the other days since he had died, he was still in the same place. There had been no change. It seemed as if two hundred years had passed since he had first become a prisoner of this strange dimension. He sometimes wondered if he were in hell.

He walked to the window of his small house, knowing what he would see. The two black suns still shone eerily bright, casting two shadows on everything their rays touched. The shadows themselves were bright, as if the light were coming from another, unseen source. Did the suns reflect moonlight here?

Here he could look directly at the suns. They were black with a thin corona. Had they not provided warmth like the one sun at home in his memory, he would have called them something else.

Daytime was infused with a peculiar shade of heightened color that actually had a smell to it. Nights were truly black and without scent. Nothing could pierce that blackness. Even a flame shone only where it danced and not a hairsbreadth further.

The lizards that wandered the streets at night, as large as full-grown wolves, provided a tasty meal, but they could see at night and felt the desires toward people. They were without wings and were known as Loping Wyverns.

He'd never gotten used to being able to see great distances in this odd light. Nonetheless, he could see as far as he might have on a clear day at home. Far on the horizon stood the ice-covered peaks of a mountain range. The peaks were craggy and made of stone. The ice covered the mountain peaks year-round. Nothing grew on those frozen mountaintops.

Every day for Daniele was much like the previous one. He felt cold. The warmth offered by the strange suns could not penetrate his bitter, cold bones. Even in light, all was darkness, and misery his only companion.

He knew that every morning there would be a trembling that would shake his house until he thought it would fall into rubble, but he was still startled when it hit, and remained terrified until it passed. Had an earthquake of that magnitude struck his beloved Venice, the city would surely have sunk into the sea. Here, nothing was laid asunder. He knew it was just the morning yawns of his terrible host, the wizard Tribuka.

Daniele took some comfort in the knowledge that the Loping Wyvern, so mighty during the night, would at dawn flee with their tails between their legs and their heads down. As far as he could tell, this dimension was eternal and the cruel wizard who ruled it was, too.

When Daniele first arrived in this strange place many years ago, he was both scared and intrigued. He explored the kingdom on the back of a dark and glacial-winged dragon. Tribuka had insisted that Daniele take this tour so he would better understand where he was and why he was there.

During some of his past journeys, beyond the perennially frozen mountain, Daniele saw Atlantis and Lemuria, as different as night and day, each a glorious testament to humankind's ingenuity. The great cities had been reduced to mere trophies for the wizard's collection. Flying onward, he saw Tritons bound to stones the size of mountains, guarding the wizard's water palace. Sirens stolen from the ocean were chained to smaller boulders, eternally singing the praises of their master. It was tortuous to Daniele's ears. The Sirens evoked a sadness from him that was so deep he did not care to know its source.

The ancient city of Troy was there, and Hercules greeted him. Hercules was adorned in a suit of armor so heavy that even he could not walk in it. The Trojan Horse sat empty in the plaza with Achilles shackled to it forever. Next, the dragon took him to the famous city of gold that Pizzaro had failed to find. The Incan king who greeted him was dressed in pure gold. Even his robes were woven of fine gold threads.

Beyond all of these famous and long-gone places of Earth were places from other worlds. At one place, Daniele met small green men with big eyes, almost miniscule ears, and long, skinny arms and legs. Their home was filled with highly advanced technological and mechanical wonders. He learned they were the only surviving race from Mars.

The final group of creatures Daniele met before returning to his little Piazza had a blue tint to their scaly skin. They had eyes like dirty coins, not as large as the ones belonging to the Martians. But they were taller than the others. They flew on tablets that emitted a blue light. They told Daniele they had come from the blue planet of the star Sirius A.

On his way back to the house where he was to spend eternity, Daniele thought about what all of these places had in common. All of them that he had known about no longer existed on the Earth plane. It dawned on him that the wizard was acquiring trophies of ancient and beautiful places. The thought both angered and terrified him.

Daniele had wondered, early on, if perhaps there was a constellation in the sky that he might recognize as a touchstone to home. He quickly learned there were no stars to see in the night's inky blackness, and the dark light of daytime didn't let any rays shine through, either. Finally, he decided that he was in a large black hole. It was the only explanation he could find for the darkness and the generally opposite nature, like he was living in a world where the negative energy was giving off light. On the Earth, light came from positive energy, he remembered. The sun was warm, but here it was cold. And yet there was light. Perhaps it was the reason such diverse civilizations from such different times and places could co-exist in this one place. The positive and the negative. Different planes of reality, like panes of glass against the night.

It had been years since Daniele had gone outside of his house for more than necessities. He ventured beyond his door to gather roots and forage for beans to make soup—or, if luck was with him, the market sometimes had Loping Wyvern meat, or the lean, tender meat of the Gryphon. Gryphon meat made a good stew.

Daniele learned quickly to carry a fat walking stick with him wherever he went, for Gryphons were known to attack humans. They could crush a skull with their talons and then take their time eating the carcass. He'd seen it once, shortly after he'd arrived. The sight haunted his nightmares still, since that day he saw one of the big birds catch up a human and eat him, tearing him into pieces. It didn't take long for him to learn to recognize a Gryphon's moving shadow above him, drop to one knee and bring the stick up in a hard arch. If he timed it right, he would have good Gryphon meat for a couple of days. If he timed it poorly, the bird would fly away for easier prey. If he wounded the Gryphon, he knew to leave it alone and move along quickly. Their cries drew others like them who would swarm the dying animal and eat it, and those who lost the battle to eat of the freshly killed prey would look around for anything else in their prevue. A human would do nicely.

On this particular day, Daniele ventured out to the main square. He has been in his house for two months and needed a change in scenery. Maybe he could find some fruit and different foods to eat. He brought some of the meat from the Gryphon he had killed the previous month, when it had come into his backyard. Perhaps he could exchange that for some different food. The market was crowded. Daniele didn't know anyone. Everyone here had been transported from previous lives, doomed to live in this condition. It seemed that the wizard had anchored their souls to this dimension so that they could not leave. The guards were a menacing presence, and the wizard of Tribuka loved to make people uncomfortable.

The rumbling of the wizard's laughter quickly engulfed the market, causing people to fall and Gryphons to crash to the ground as they attempted to make a kill. Daniele knew that the wizard only laughed when he was about to acquire another trophy. He felt a bit guilty for hoping it was not from Earth.

When he heard a choir of angels performing strains of Monteverdi's *Magnificat*, he fell to his knees, sobbing. When alive, he had freed Venice from the Austrian empire, setting the stage for Italian autonomy, which set forth the year after his death. Now he learned that his fight had been for nothing. His home, the place he had always held dear to his heart, was soon to be condemned to eternity in this dark, unforgiving, infinite chamber of desolation.

He hurried home. He had to figure out a way to warn his city, to prepare them to fight, though this foe appeared unconquerable. Upon arriving at his home, he heard the voice of the wizard.

"Come to me now, Manin. It is time you knew why you are here. Perhaps you can save your fair city, but I doubt it."

The Frost Dragon landed behind him and waited, lowering itself and twisting its tail to make a footboard so that Manin could mount it for the flight to the wizard's castle.

As the dragon lifted smoothly and rapidly into the dark sky, his yellow eyes burned bright, surveying everything, and clouds of smoke spewed from his nostrils.

Sitting on the dragon's neck, Manin considered his options. He had nothing to lose. He could not die again, and living in this place was worse than death. Whatever should happen to him, he could not let the same fate befall his beloved Venice.

CHAPTER 15

A FROST FUTURE

"*Manin, do not make me wait,*" repeated the Wizard Tribuka, suppressing a laugh. "*Perhaps you can save your fair city, but probably not.*"

At the sound of his laughter, all other sounds were drowned out. It seemed as though every time he laughed something terrible was going to happen. Manin knew that, too, and began to shiver, from the fear of something terrible and unstoppable happening. Venice was in danger. He could think of no other explanation. He climbed onto the back of the Frost Dragon and flew to the wizard's castle.

The castle was a made of rock and ice. It was a mountain frozen within an iceberg. The dragon dropped him in from of the front door. It was big enough for the dragon to walk through, but not even a frost dragon wanted to go inside that castle.

Manin got off the dragon and walked inside. The gray, stone walls were painted with different scenes. Some portrayed a figure in a blue cloak waving his hands before different cities. Others portrayed the same cloaked figure laughing as he watched the same cities experience catastrophes like earthquakes, meteor showers or lightning storms. Then Manin saw a painting of what could only be the Wizard's palace with the same cities before they were taken to Tribuka. He soon realized that those were the memories of the Wizard's accomplishments. Manin looked closer at the scenes. There was Tribuka with Attila the Hun, and there was Tribuka in Atlantis. Even in the picture, it was more beautiful than he had imagined. He knew that the real city was somewhere inside the infinite world of Tribuka. Was that world in a parallel dimension or in a different galaxy? The picture of Lemuria followed and then Babylonia. Manin shuddered. Had Lemuria sunk? Did it ever exist? Was it a lost land somewhere between the Indian and the Pacific Ocean? Mauritia and the Kerguelen Plateau in the Indian Ocean do exist, but there is no known geological formation under the Indian or Pacific Oceans that could have served as a land bridge between continents.

He stopped since he saw a strong and beautiful light coming to from the streets of that lost town. He went close and noticed an amazing crystal of Lemurian Quartz. The legend said that this quartz could heal any disease. What a strange light it had. But wait, there were many all around the city. What a beautiful scene of lights and serenity. Serenity, not really, since he was in Tribuka Castle and the wizard was waiting for him. All of these beautiful places were stolen from the worlds where they were built.

He saw another scene of Babylonia, and noticed a long line of people walking around the castle of Babylonia, from the bottom going around in a circle to reach the top. It seems that the Babylonians were there still, chained together under the watchful eye of Tribuka commanders. Tribuka had stolen the inhabitants as well as their home.

What a pity for those people, Manin thought. Then he noticed a magnificent city that appeared to be built on a set of canals. A tall tower, two more setting up the time, a cathedral with racing horse and ... wait a minute that was Venice. His heart and his jaw dropped. It was undeniable. The image before him was of Venezia, his home.

If Venice is on the wall, he thought, Then that must mean...

He hurried through the castle corridor, not even stopping to look at the remainder of the paintings. He soon found himself in the great hall where the wizard spent his days. A rumor spread that Tribuka was traveling all the time, seeking places to add to his collections.

A large wooden table with enormous chairs stood in the middle, wine odors were still emanating from it, but otherwise it was clean. Maybe there was a big party here. Why? There were no other signs, and definitely, there were no signs of women's presence. Probably just a business meeting. but to discuss what, and with whom?

As Manin thought about it, Tribuka was in fact, a collector. Yes, like people collected paintings, coins, or stamps, the wizard was collecting places from around the galaxy. Why was he allowed to do that? Allowed by whom? He did not know the answer.

"Finally, you are here," the wizard boomed loudly, shaking Manin to his core. "I summoned you here because your town is soon to be mine!" He laughed. "I am a good wizard, you know. When I see something I want, I get it, but I don't take it by force. No, I make deals with the inhabitants. If they hold up their end of the deal, they can keep their home, but I take it if they don't, and they never do." The wizard's eyes glittered. "Yes, a long time ago I wanted your spectacular Venice, but I made a deal with the Venetians. See, I admire humans. You have built such wonderful things. I respect your work. I would think, 'if these humans are so amazing and able to build such wonders, perhaps they deserve to keep them too.' So when I first saw Venice and its people, I wanted it, but I said, 'If you can love and appreciate your home, it will remain yours.' I gave you and your people a chance to build it and to preserve it. Everybody thinks I am malignant. But who is worse? I who take the gifts discarded like trash by unappreciative owners, or the owners who reject these precious gifts?" He waved his arms as if he were orchestrating an opera.

"Before I take a city, I make sure to bring one of the city's heroes here with me to give you humans an even better chance to redeem yourselves. Yes, you guessed correctly. Time, for Venice, is running out. But I am giving you, Manin, a chance to contact someone in your town and see if you can save it. I enjoy this game. But in the end, it is not really a game. I want people to understand the value of what they have and to take care of it. If you have a son or a daughter or a partner, you need to take care of them. Otherwise they will leave you. Likewise, if you can't take care of your city, it will leave you, or, I suppose, I will take it." The wizard chuckled.

Manin shivered at the sound of it

"Truthfully," continued the wizard, "I am the defender of the most beautiful cities in the world. Who is it that preserves years of splendor and prosperity, years of glorious history against the disease of human stupidity? Me. Just me. I am the paladin of beauty. If the human race or other races cannot take care of their city, I will take it and add it to my collection. Here it shall remain, preserved in my collection until a new generation of gentle people is born. If there is a generation who can appreciate their city's beauty more than I do, they can have it back. However," he sneered, "they never, ever do. Once a place is mine, it is mine forever." He rubbed his hands in gleeful anticipation and continued.

"Humankind has been very disappointing. Don't get me wrong. I like humans. I like their energy, their sensitivity, their love, and their hate. I like their capability to build and destroy, to cry and to fight. They, or should I say, you, have passion. But you and your fellow humans are stupid and do not always recognize the value in what you have. You do not take care of their gifts and instead, ruin them. Now perhaps *you* are different. Heroic, you were for your people, and I respect it and want to give you the last chance to try to save them. Go to your place. Try to find someone to contact, and I will allow you to talk to that person. I will not interfere with your job. It is more-or-less an impossible mission, but I am giving you a chance anyway." The Wizard smiled confidently. "I hope you will manage to find someone who cares."

With those words, the conversation ended abruptly. The wizard stood at his full height, and with a small gesture of his hand, made himself disappear.

Manin stood there alone. He heard a noise in the closest room. The frost dragon was spreading the wings and making that flapping sound, a sign they need to go. Reluctantly, Manin climbed on, and the dragon took him to his house.

During the flight, he was thinking about Venice. He saw frosted towns, one after another, and one in Tribuka he could not even recognize. Maybe the altitude of the flight, maybe the frost encompassing it all. But he did not want that to happen to his beloved Venice.

———

When Daniele arrived at his house, he went promptly to his bed and sat with legs crossed and hands opened toward the sky in a meditation posture. Before that, he burned some old herbs he had been collecting with the power to enhance meditation and transport the soul across time zones. He was trying to channel his entire mental capacity towards finding a champion within his mother city. He needed to transport his soul back to earth immediately. Would he be successful? He didn't know but had to try.

CHAPTER 16

DANIELE MANIN AND VENICE'S FREEDOM

Walking home from university, Marco decided to take the short way through the Ponte dell' Accademia. After crossing over the bridge, he found himself in Campo Santo Stefano when he heard someone calling his name.

"Marco!"

It was Viviana Ancona, his friend from school.

"How are you doing? Long time, no see."

"Hello," replied Marco, coming closer to kiss her twice on each cheek. "What are you up to these days?"

"My parents are super busy, they just opened a restaurant in the ghetto and they are doing very well. We are doing a lot of weddings and ceremonies like Bar Mitzvahs. It seems there are a lot of young boys in Venice!" She started laughing, a good laugh. Now Marco remembered what he liked about her. It was that laugh—full-blown and showing perfect teeth between full lips. Marco laughed, too.

"You have to tell me about yourself," she continued. "Still busy with the university? Still trying to save Venice?" She took his arm under hers. "Let's get a cicheto. I need to eat something. I eat little but often!" She laughed again.

"I know a good place around here. Let's go," said Marco.

Viviana was so full of life she gave energy in every word she was saying. She would be a good friend and companion, but Marco knew she was already engaged to one of the prominent member sons of the ghetto. This energy was just what he needed now. The hatred and violence of the riot still weighed heavily on his mind.

As they walked through San Stefano, Marco stopped for a second.

"Look, Viviana, this is one of my favorite campos. It is large and you can sit outside and play soccer."

She laughed. "I don't play soccer," she teased.

"You have no idea how many times I played here when I was little since it's not far from my house. Look at this! In my opinion, this well is still one of the most beautiful structures in all Venice." Marco pointed to the large well in the campo, no longer in use, but that still served as a reminder of how many people had been able to use it, due to its size.

The two passed by the well and took a little calle on the left, where there was a Bacaro. The place had a large window door, and once they entered, Marco could see the old barrel tables. There was a display counter made of glass laden beneath with favorite dishes.

"I will get a squid, ten smelts, sardines with onions and raisins and an octopus," said Viviana "What about you?"

"I will get some baccala alla Vicentina, and how I like it—cooked with milk, and sardines, too, in *saor* and yes, two squids. Viviana, they have some fresh Recioto del Soave! Let's get two glasses of that."

Vivian nodded in agreement. They started with the wine, a good white, light wine, and they finished before the food was ready. They ordered another one. Wine was not a problem when eating, as the food settled the wine glow. They were eating and talk catching up on old times when they were in high school together.

"How is architecture, Viviana? You like your classes?'"

"It is great. We learn so much stuff, it's unbelievable. I want to be an interior designer and the other day I was very impressed by Frank Lloyd Wright. I like his houses! I like the designs of the structures, the harmony they exude, and the feeling inside of them. Like they have humanity, and that expands to fill their environment. You know, a philosopher, I don't remember his name, called it, organic architecture."

Marco laughed "I thought that organic only referred to fruits and vegetables. It is interesting, to be sure."

"What are *you* up to, then?" asked Viviana. "I read your article in the *Gazzettino*. That, of course, is how I know you are still doing all you can to save Venice."

"I am trying," he said gravely. "But I have a sinking feeling that something terrible will happen. I cannot explain what it is. People are so detached from the environment where they live that it seems they can live in any place or on any planet, and it will not make any difference, as far as the place gives to them what they need. They don't understand that they have to give something over to the town before the town gives something back to them."

"I agree it is unbelievable. Even in my field. There are people who want everything from the house. They call interior designers to fix them and then they don't take care of *the place* itself. They probably think that their expensive designer will take care of them."

"Right, " replied Marco. They finished their food their wine, and he was lost in thought about what she had said.

While they were paying the bill, Vivian asked him, "What do you think about that racist riot that occurred the other day? I cannot believe that a fair strike with fair demands for work hours and better working conditions went that direction. You know our community always monitored those issues before, and now, something is different."

"I agree," said Marco as they walked outside. "I am always wondering why a person's religion, place of birth, or skin color would matter at all."

The day was still young. The canals were lit by the sun, and as they walked together, Campo San Stefano square was full of life. People sat at tables outside enjoying the day with light lunches and spritzer aperitifs. Children were playing soccer nearby. It was joyful to see the simple pleasures of life in action on such a beautiful summer day in Venice. It was not too hot, even for the end of August. A perfect time to have a walk and enjoy the enchantment of the town.

"I cannot be more in agreement with you," Viviana continued, "that at a time of using the religion to excuse their own business, religion should be above daily human interest, should be detached from the heart's desire and be considered above all. It should not matter what religion a person practices! Why should it? If I have to build a house or design one, does it matter if I am Jewish or Catholic or Muslim? No! You should judge me for my work only." She stopped, having run out of breath at the end of her sentence.

"I agree with you," said Marco. "We are often judged by our religion, race, or appearance, and our job and ideals become secondary."

"I have to go to San Zaccaria, so I'll walk with you."

"Okay, let's go. I am heading home."

They arrived in Campo Manin in front of Marco's house, and sat on the steps of the statue. Marco continued the conversation. "Did you know he was a Jew?"

"Really?" Viviana raised her eyebrows and straightened up, giving her the appearance of being taller than she was.

"Many people who were being so hateful claim loyalty to the memory of Daniele Manin, yet they don't seem to remember that he was born Daniele Bellotto. He was an adult when he took the name of Manin, in honor of Lodovico Manin, who had sponsored his grandfather's conversion from Judaism to Christianity in 1759." He chuckled. "I guess I really am a living, breathing historical paper. But there's irony. One of Venice's greatest heroes descended from Jews."

Still seated at the foot of the statue of Manin, they rested and reflected.

"I can't believe that people would not know something like that," said Viviana. "Or perhaps I can. I myself never paid that much attention in history. Refresh my memory, then. What happened with the Austrian and Manin?"

"If Manin had one flaw," Marco started, "it was his unabashed and deeply held hatred for Austria, which he had carried from his youth. Manin spent a short time in prison due to his hatred of Austria when he petitioned the Venetian congregation to tell the Austrian emperor of the needs of the nation. The charge was high treason. From January 18, 1848, to March 17 of the same year, he was in prison. That same year, Venice revolted. Fortunately for Manin, the revolution was not going well for Austria, and Venice forced Count Pallfy, the Austrian governor, to release Manin. Soon Austria lost control of the city, and Manin led a revolution which removed the last of them."

"Unbelievable," said Vivian "He did this single-handedly, and he was not even born in Venice? I am starting to like him now even better since I now know he was a Jew." She laughed her beautiful laugh. The way her lips made a circle of her mouth, showing those white teeth, it was as if her body was laughing along with her when she was laughing. She was one body and one laugh.

Marco continued. "Manin became president of the newly re-created Republic of San Marco on March 26, the day the of Austrians withdrew from Venice. He resigned on August 7 that same year to allow annexation to Piedmont, which he did not favor but knew was the only chance for unification at that time. The Piedmontese was not to last, however, and they quickly abandoned , Venice to Austria. Austria had reinforced troops and had reoccupied all of the Venetian mainlands. The citizenry had had enough. Giving all they had in worldly goods, in fighting determination and in spirit, the people's cry was 'Resistance at all costs!' Manin became the president of the Republic and was granted unlimited powers.

"A living, breathing essay," she laughed.

Marco blushed, but continued as he was in a heat of oral passion. "The fight continued until supplies were nearly used up and Manin negotiated a settlement with terms which included amnesty to all save himself and Neapolitan general, Guglielmo Pepe. The two of them were to go into exile forever. On August 27, Manin left Italy forever aboard a French ship. In 1868, two years after the Austrians finally departed Venice, Manin's remains were brought to his native city and honored with a public funeral. His remains are interred in a sarcophagus in the Piazzetta dei Leoncini, on the north side of the Basilica San Marco." Marco pointed to something far in the distance, a direction only.

Marco never tired of reliving the story of Daniele Manin. It inspired him, and he dreamed of living through it. They had such a good time that afternoon, but it was turning to its end.

Viviana started. "I have to go! Gosh, I am late! I have to pick up something for my dad. Need to get there before the shop closes."

They kissed each other on the cheek, and she left.

Marco went home still thinking about the conversation. He had had a good afternoon with the laughing one who listened to history so patiently.

"Marco, who was there? Was that Viviana?" asked his mother.

"Yes," Marco said. "We were just catching up, such a long time since I last saw her."

"She is a fine girl," added his mother, who had known Viviana from Marco's high school days as well. She wanted to say more, but Marco could tell she was restraining herself, as her lips pursed.

"Are you hungry? I have made some artichoke hearts and risotto with mushroom."

"I love artichokes. Great," said Marco.

"I am home," called Marco's father from downstairs who had just arrived from work. "What is that delicious smell? Fantastic."

They sat at the table and Marco's father opened a Soave white wine.

"I heard that they have the names of those people who caused the riot the other day. I hope they catch them. It was a shame for the whole of Venice," said his father.

"We cannot tolerate this in Venice. Otherwise, we are losing all our principles of freedom, and then what would Manin say?" Marco said, striking a pose like hero in the statue nearby.

They all laughed good-naturedly and finished their dinner. After watching a little TV show, Marco went to his room. He realized that he did not have his valet. He looked for it but could not find it. His parents were in bed already, and Marco got dressed and went out to see if he had dropped it somewhere.

There it was. Marco was happy to see it. It lay at the base of the statue where he was sitting earlier. He sat there for a short time, relieved it was still there.

He felt someone near him, and was so lost in trying to decipher the feeling that he didn't notice the statue now sitting directly in front of him— it had moved on its own.

CHAPTER 17

THE CONVERSATION FROM OUT OF SPACE

"You remind me of a younger version of myself," said Manin.

At last, he was able to get in touch with someone. Tribuka allowed him to do so. He moved his soul into his own statue to talk to Marco, his young friend.

The man looked bronze, his green patina flat against the falling dusk. Marco tentatively and gingerly tapped his knuckle against the man's knee. It rang like bronze. The man smiled understandingly.

"If it helps you to believe you're dreaming, go ahead," the statue said. "But hear me. I have watched you grow up in the house I was born in. For almost 100 years, my soul has been wondering in a frozen world. At the time I was able to escape and hide in my statue. During these last few years I noticed many things, but I could not talk. I've watched you grow into a strong, intelligent, compassionate, and patriotic young man. Until recently, I could not speak to you, although I've wanted to. I see the same passion in you that I once carried. If anyone can save Venice, it is you."

Marco held up his hand with his palm facing the statue of Manin. The bronze man folded his hands in his lap, closed his mouth, and waited patiently.

"Continue," said Marco.

Manin smiled. "*Grazie.* You were so preoccupied with your worries that you did not notice the changes in me. Look at me now, Marco. See the wrinkles of worry, see the tracks of my tears—I've been weeping for our beloved Venice for at least a century."

As Manin spoke these words, Marco remembered dreams that he'd had of the man. In those dreams, the Manin had been sitting on the front steps of his house crying disconsolately. Then, as he would do mindless chores or errands, he would see Manin in his mind's eye, pleading with the ancient Gods, petitioning sorcerers of all kinds to wake the people of Venice up and motivate them to care for their home again. Marco remembered how every time he ranted about the lazy hubris that had come to characterize the city, he would feel as though he was actually Manin, himself. All of those dreams and visions, somehow, had been suppressed until now. As they came together in his mind, he realized what was happening and that it was real this time. The spirit of Daniele Manin was occupying a bronze statue that was now talking with him. He realized at that moment that it was a pivotal moment in the history of Venice and that it would never be put down in the history books. He knew what he had to do now.

"I am ready now," he told Manin. "I am ready to hear what you have to say." The statue smiled gently. There was a fondness in his eyes for the young man.

"I have known from the first time I saw you as an infant," Manin spoke, "that you were the one we've been waiting for all these years. The other watchers, statues all around Venice, did not want me to reach out to you. They feared you would not respond well. I told them that I knew you better than any of them, and that I knew you could indeed handle this if given time to adjust to the reality of it. I told them that your love of Venice was greater than even my own. I told them that your inquisitiveness made you open to the seemingly impossible and that you would allow yourself to listen to my words, that you would not concentrate on the absence of a scientific explanation for it. I can see that I was correct in this way of thinking."

Marco began to relax. His studies in philosophy and his conversations with many philosophers and teachers, like professor Grassi, the mayor, and more, had made of his mind a malleable, yet disciplined organ that would serve him perfectly in this time. Manin was right. He would heed the message without judging the way it was given.

"The waters of Venice in the early years," Manin began, "were crystal clear. You could use it as a mirror. Fish were plentiful. Fruits and vegetables grew readily on the island. Venice was Eden. The people were happy, simple folk who had no ambitions beyond enjoying life and loving each other. They were good neighbors. They built strong families. Morgan le Fay came to Venice many times over the centuries. She had fallen in love with it. When she brought Merlin with her, he was impressed with the beauty and the good-hearted nature of the people."

Marco's eyes grew wide at the mention of Morgan le Fay, the Sorceress, and of Merlin, the greatest wizard that ever lived. He leaned in to listen to Manin, enchanted by every word.

CHAPTER 18

ATTILA THE HUN

"Attila the Hun had heard of Venice from his emissary, the evil wizard Tribuka," Manin continued. "The emissary told Attila of Venice's beauty and her wonders. However, Attila did not know that his emissary was the evil wizard Tribuka, the most powerful wizard ever to come to Earth from another dimension, who served no master except himself. Attila thought that he was working for him, but Tribuka was manipulating him. He thought Tribuka was his servant, not his master. The Hun was not a bright man, but he was a brilliant fighter. He decided to conquer Venice and to add it to his empire. He did not understand that his very presence destroyed beautiful things."

"How any man would like to destroy beautiful things, I don't get it," said Marco. "Was Attila's only goal to destroy and not to build?"

Manin nodded. "Everywhere Attila went, he left devastation in his wake. His need to possess beautiful things was greater than his capacity to care for them. When the Venetians caught wind of the Hun's present ambition to conquer their city, they invoked the help of Morgan le Fay."

Marco had heard of this legend, but he had never heard the story in its entirety. "Please tell me more? What did Morgan do?" He hoped Manin would not skip any details.

"The Hun's army was sweeping a path of destructive victory toward Venice that had the people terrified," Manin said. "They had better weapons than anyone had ever seen before. Each soldier was rumored to have the strength of ten men. As fantastic as it all sounded, Attila's outstanding victories could not be denied, or ignored for that matter. Morgan le Fay learned that Attila had the help of the wizard Tribuka, who was using his gifts to ensure that the Hun conquered every land he attacked."

"Who is this wizard? I never heard about him."

"Tribuka is a powerful wizard, and probably the most powerful that nobody knows about him and when they do, it is the last thing they know."

The statue moved his arm and Marco thought he heard a slight rasping sound.

"Tribuka," said Manin, "was using Attila's ambition to help him steal the most beautiful places on Earth. He would cause a terrible natural disaster and make the lands seem to disappear when in reality he was taking them back to his back to his world. Tribuka had been collecting beautiful lands from countless worlds in the universe."

"His universe?" Marco scoffed. "Can someone have his own universe?"

"Oh, but yes, it is possible. Tribuka did not care about the people of the lands he wanted. To him, people were as livestock, only there to serve a purpose as he saw fit. He thought nothing of killing them or of putting them in harm's way if it served his purposes. He saw himself as a practical man, and he took no pleasure in destruction, though it caused him no grief either. His only saving grace was that he never harmed for harm's sake because there was no practical value to such a thing. However, the Hun and his men frequently did, so together they caused much strife."

"So what happened then?"

"Morgan le Fay and Merlin decided to try to reason with the wizard. If the Hun wasn't a part of the negotiation, there was a chance they could save Venice, or at least buy her time. Unfortunately, the wizard of Tribuka was known for his determination. Morgan le Fay had little doubt that eventually he would take Venice as his own. But she was going to try her best to save it for as long as she could. She told the people of Venice to move into the lagoon islands. Attila was taking land before the people of Venice could hide. The little islands in the lagoon had countless well-known natural hiding places, from caves to grottoes to wooded areas, but it was too late to run. He had arrived much faster than expected. Tribuka knew that Attila was no sailor, so he had taken the islands closest to the mainland, where the sweetest fruits grew."

"That is why they left the land and came to the lagoon?" asked Marco. "They knew Attila was not comfortable with water battles."

"Exactly," replied Manin. "Merlin and Morgan le Fay went to the island of Murano. There they summoned Tribuka, using his vanity. Murano is where the finest glass and mirrors are made because the silica is so pure. Tribuka could not resist a perfect mirror, and they knew it. While Tribuka was at Murano enamored by his reflection, the Venetian people were fighting the Hun's army with all they had. They used the advantages that knowing the land and the waters gave them. They used trickery whenever possible. They were even able to take advantage of a couple of Fata Morgana mirages to confuse the hordes while they set up some traps. Merlin had cast some preparatory spells to help them win the day."

"And they all were in Murano together. What about the battles?"

"Merlin and Tribuka watched the battles together through hand-made telescopes with lenses fashioned from Murano's finest glass," said Manin. "The ingenuity and compassion showed by the Venetians, always returning to save the wounded, sacrificing themselves for a friend, even running suicide missions to destroy enemy positions did not go unnoticed by either wizard. They also saw the Hun's horde was killing without care or notice. If one of their own was injured, they were left to fend for themselves or die. They attacked men, women, children, and animals with equally destructive gusto. They cared not who suffered or who were left behind— their blood-lust was monstrous, their focus machine-like."

"That was terrible," said Marco. "How did they settle it?"

"Close your eyes, Marco. I will take you to the moment when Merlin and Tribuka sat down to negotiate the fate of Venice."

CHAPTER 19

THE DEAL WITH
TRIBUKA THE WIZARD

Marco closed his eyes. When he opened them a second later, he was at once on the ancient island of Murano. It was clean and beautiful—green with fertile, rich-looking soil and plant life sprouting up between buildings. All the houses were shining, reflecting the sunrise, thanks to the famous glass that at that time was used to make the windows of the houses. He could see peach orchards and a large winery. Sheep roamed together with cows. Large trees towered over the scene, obscuring the distant lands.

His awe was magnified when he saw the presence of the two wizards standing side-by-side, looking out over the battle that Marco could just hear. Neither man was unusually tall. Neither man was young. Both were strong and healthy and stood with the ease and grace of one long accustomed to having a hard-working body. Each was handsome in his own way. Merlin had gentle eyes, deep-set and strikingly blue, eyes that told tales of ancient days long ago when magic reigned in the cosmos. Tribuka had striking green eyes and dark hair shot through with gray at the temples, and he sported a carefully trimmed goatee. His vanity was clear to see and not without justification. Neither man seemed to see Marco.

"It would be a waste to let the Venetian people be slaughtered," Merlin offered to his fellow wizard. "Their souls are so much more advanced, the gifts they bring to the world are so much more beautiful and useful than that which the Hun's hordes have to give."

"The hordes have no souls," said Tribuka. "They are a hive of pure panic and chaos set to accomplish one thing—destroy everything they find and keep moving forward. They have done enough damage."

With that, Tribuka waved a hand over the horizon where the battle was taking place, and the action froze as if it were a painting.

Morgan le Fay appeared in front of the wizards and stepped up to face them. Marco could not figure where she had come from. She seemed to have just appeared out of the ether. Her long black hair waved in what seemed to be wind, and her green eyes flashed.

"I am pleased to see that you share my love for this place and these people," she said to Tribuka. "Perhaps we can work together to preserve it, and them, in a manner that would appease your hunger."

When Morgan le Fay said the word "hunger", something in her bearing changed slightly, and she looked severe and decisive, her eyes darkened into a smoky gray. She reminded Marco of a shark. Marco was enchanted with Morgan le Fay's beauty. Indeed, she was a beauty as he had ever seen, with her raven black hair, her deep and large green eyes, her high, sharp cheekbones and full red lips. She wouldn't need to sing to force a sailor to crash his ship. All she would need to do is stand in his sight, and he would lose all sense. He knew already he was in love with her and looking at her now confirmed it. He was hoping she was indeed the owner of the book he found in the museum the other day.

"Your people, Morgan le Fay," Tribuka responded, "are rare and precious. They value life, but they do not fear either sacrifice or death. They can create with a genius unparalleled, and yet they can destroy without a second thought. It is clear to me that they adore you. These people are truly your children in spirit. I have an offer for you. For now, I will leave you the lagoon, the islands, and the people. The Hun will turn his hordes away and march on once I free them. They will do no more harm. However, you must keep this place as the most beautiful place on Earth with its unique beauty from the core of the people's hearts to the surface of the land. You must defend it as if it were your child, much as you did today, with intelligence and heart. Venice must be a republic and never a tyranny, and this is why I do not take it for myself. I wear the yoke of a tyrant with pride, and I know a tyrant would destroy this place. You must protect it from the weather. You must protect it from an imbalance in nature. There is no negotiation. Either they preserve it, or I will eventually take it away." Tribuka's visage turned dark, his smile sinister.

"But there is one fate it is destined for," he continued. "And when that fate comes to pass, I shall return and I will take Venice to be my own. When indifference and apathy replace the passion and love that is now the people's legacy, then the city will decay. The buildings will fall into disrepair and collapse. There will be a stench upon the waters, and they shall reek of urine and garbage. The people will starve, for there will be no fish to eat. The people who are now as siblings will become like strangers to each other. They will be governed by greed, and they will have no regard for anything but their selfish desires. Then I shall return, and I will take Venice to be my kingdom. I will take the buildings, the squares, the bridges, and the souls." He waved his arms in an imperial fashion.

"The few who still love and care will live eternally in the square of St. Mark. There they will have all that they need to create, to learn and to continue to grow, for one day they will want to take their Venice back, and if they can once again learn to love their city, they can have it back." He smirked. "But I guarantee that won't happen. Just as the dead cannot reclaim their former lives once they have passed, once apathy ensnares the human mind, it never lets go. That which is dead remains dead."

He took a breath, then exhaled, and the foulness of the air increased.

"The remainder and majority of souls in the city will be dull and dumb. They will have no sense of self, no sense of community, no sense of responsibility. These souls will become eternal slaves to me. All souls belonging to Venice will be weighed accordingly, and regardless of where they live, they will come to their destiny at my hands. From today until that day Venice shall be known as *La Serenissima Repubblica di Venezia*. The Serene Republic of Venice. Only the Paladins of Venice, those who fight for her, will be freed when I return. They will go out into the world with a warning message to all who would be indifferent, dull, and dumb."

With that, Tribuka laughed—long and low and full of malice. "Merlin, one day Venice will be mine."

Merlin nodded sadly.

"Alas," Tribuka continued. "From what I've learned of the nature of man, you will indeed capture Venice in your snare, and it might not be all that long before you do. For humanity cycles from caring deeply to hardly noticing his surroundings. There will come a day when the dullards outnumber the brilliant ones."

"Over my dead body," Morgan le Fay offered defiantly.

"It brings me no pleasure to agree with you, my lady," Tribuka responded with a somber bow. "That, too, must come to pass."

Morgan le Fay swore to continue to inspire and defend Venice for as long as she lived. And Merlin swore that he would always to help her as she needed.

And with a wave of his hand, Tribuka allowed the battle to resume. The horde stopped, turned and retreated. With no warning and seemingly for no reason, the Huns, who just a minute ago seemed hell-bent on conquest, and who just a minute ago could not be reasoned with, departed. The Venetians were dumbfounded, but wary. They could not believe what they had just seen, but the suffering of the wounded could not be ignored or postponed. They took the opportunity to recover as best as they could.

Once the hordes had gone, Morgan le Fay froze her people one more time. She returned to Venice to its beauty of just a day before. She healed those who had been injured. She could not raise the dead, but she could alter the memories of the living so that it did not feel like slaughter, but rather a challenge that was now behind them. Remembering her promise to Tribuka, Morgan le Fay became Venice's high protector, guarding her throughout the years against invaders.

CHAPTER 20

THE FAITH OF VENICE

"Marco, open your eyes now."

As much as he wanted to stay on that beautiful island, Marco opened his eyes.

"How long have I been gone?"

"Eternity and one minute."

"I need to know more," said Marco, who for some reason had shameful tears in his eyes.

"You've heard the legend that Morgan le Fay died in Sicily," Manin stated. "If you look at the history of Venice, our protectress Morgan le Fay passed from this world shortly before the republic died. That's when things started going downhill. It is a common legend that Merlin outlived Morgan le Fay. I believe this is so. He would have been weak and old, but perhaps his magic bought us a bit more time in hopes that we might make it through. Even so, our time may well be up, my young friend. The duty has fallen upon you to try."

Marco felt overcome with hopelessness. "I am no wizard, Signore Manin, but a mere student," "Who am I to save Venice?"

"For over a thousand years," Manin said, "parents told their children of the magnificence and the uniqueness of our city. Her history, legend, and lore were all woven together in those stories just as they always have been in her daily activities. But in the last two centuries, those stories have faded. At first, the stories of the magic were separated and told as fairy tales. The age of reason had begun to infect the minds of Venetians, and they could no longer believe that magic was real. Over the generations, those stories ceased to have meaning. Only our documented and logical history remain, and most people have decided that it is boring or too long to tell. They have no pride even in the stories anymore. Barely anybody knows of the Wizard of Tribuka, or of Morgan le Fay, who tried to help the people keep their city and to save us from his curse. At night, those who listen can hear the faint sound of the Tribuka's evil laugh as he prepares to take Venice into slavery. The people of Venice were once courageous. They were creators. They were geniuses. They awed the Gods themselves. They were able to discover the new way to China with Marco Polo, they built ships which were faster and stronger than any other. They were good diplomats and able to conduct good trade around the Mediterranean. They formed a republic before anyone in the world did, and a court system when in other countries, the people were killed for no reason. This all occurred from a small area on the Adriatic Sea, a little town compared to other large countries and nations they had to deal with. I guess they were hard workers and God blessed them. But now, they are sloppy and scared and blame others for their fears. No longer do Venetians think of amassing wealth for all. Now it is only for themselves. They have forgotten that when one rises, we all rise. And when one falls, we all fall."

"Marco, you can tell the stories," Manin said to the young man. "You can revive the legends. You can remind the old men what they once knew was true, and they can help you teach the young men. It may be too late for Venice, but maybe there is still time. You have to try. Try to talk to people, go and visit the mayor again, write more articles. Do something before it is too late."

Marco frowned. "I thought Italian unification would have gotten rid of this problem."

Manin shook his head, as the statue began to lose its pliancy.

CHAPTER 21

VENICE IS DYING

"I don't have much time, and neither do you," the statue said. "For years we used to have two doges, heads of state, to lead us. Then there were wars, and we had traitors sell us out for a few *zecchini*. They took over and sold Venice. We were such a courageous people, at one time we hosted Jews during the Nazi occupation. We always gave splendorous light to the Italian Republic. But unification was not the answer that I had hoped it would be. As in all countries, only a few men have real courage. Those men should always be the leaders because most men will follow them and will do good and courageous things. They believe in the doges. The men who follow the brave will stand up, and often they do so blindly, but it is not fear that motivated them, it was hope, for a better government." Manin paused, and what looked like a wet drop formed in the corner of his eye. He tried to shake it away. The effort was in vain, as his bronze was hardening.

He continued. "But a coward can appear brave when he is just a bully, and that is what happened to us. Cowards convinced the average man to fear his neighbor, to fear the loss of even the least consequential things. Men who are fighting among themselves will never fight for their freedom from outside oppressors. They will not take pride in the homes they jealously protect, and so their lives become sour, and their homes become as cesspools containing the worst of them and repulsing the best."

"I have seen this," Marco reflected.

"So you have. Freedom is never easy to maintain, and it is never free. But cowards will tell you that freedom is found in fearing your brother much like current politicians who attempt to make fear of immigrants create a false solution to their economic problems, and most people will believe whatever they are told. They cannot see that the freedom of one man in a community is not enough. All must be free, or all are enslaved. When men believe these lies, war, destruction, and corruption grow. Eventually, everyone becomes jaded. They expect the worst of their leaders, and so when they get the worst, they don't hold those leaders accountable. Fathers no longer teach their sons about civic service. They now teach them how to get other people to do the work for them. Even worse, they teach their sons that if nobody does what is needed, maybe it is not necessary after all. Now the city seems to feel that even basic cleanliness is unnecessary."

The tear that had formed in the corner of the statue's eye now ran down the bronze cheek. Manin didn't wipe it away. Marco assumed he had grown accustomed to the feeling.

"Since the death of our beloved Goldoni," Manin said, "the city has slowly but surely fallen into ruin. It was as if his life contained the last remnant of the pure Venetian creative force. I've long suspected that he was the last Venetian to receive the blessing of Morgan le Fay before her death. I do not think it was a coincidence that only four years after his death, Venice ceased to be a republic. How could we have ever beaten France and Austria if we did not believe in ourselves? How could we unify with all of Italy and still fall apart? Vandals steal chunks of plaster wall.

Building foundations are left to crack and crumble, the water is dark and infested. Venice is decaying right before our eyes."

"What can we do?" Marco asked.

Manin looked down at the young man and wavered. "The Wizard of Tribuka will exact his will upon us. When he cast his curse, he based it in the most certain thing he could, human nature. No creature has ever been so creative, so inventive, so brilliant in ways to destroy itself as mankind has."

"How is Venice's future even salvageable?" Marco asked. "Can we do nothing to save her?"

Manin craned his neck noisily to the night sky. "You are our final hope, Marco. You must get the people to love their city again. We have so much to do. Restructuring, restorations, cleaning the canals, we need to block the high tide with a project that will work. Mostly, what we need is love for our city. If we all love Venice again, we will fix this, and the Wizard of Tribuka will be denied the realization of his evil plan. If we can love Venice, perhaps she will feel it. She may love us back. She suffers in silence and can do nothing without love. If we fail, millions of souls will be lost for eternity in slavery to Tribuka. Only a few will live on in the Piazza San Marco to try and build again, but with the wizard going against you, it will take an eternity. Go! Shout it to the four corners of our fair city, Marco! Come back to me in thirty days, and we will see what we need to do."

The statue of Daniele Manin stood with a rusty groan, gave Marco one final nod, and resumed his position on the pedestal, freezing in place as if he had never left it. Marco sat on the step in front of the statue for a few minutes more, letting everything he had just experienced soak in.

He felt immense gratitude that Manin was still his ally. Throughout his life, he had appealed and begged the statue to guide him, to advise him on how he could save Venice, but his pleas were always left unanswered. No one, not Manin, nor anyone else, ever responded to him. Marco for the longest time had wanted to be heard. Had his moment finally arrived? Had someone finally heard him? He knew it had—he was sure of it. It must have. There was no way it couldn't have. Manin had reminded Marco that he still had work to do. He would not let the young man decide that this had all been a bad dream. Marco stood staring at the statue for a long moment. He saw the resolve on Manin's face. He looked down at the lion. It was eager to take flight and carry the message of unity, civic duty, and love to everyone who would listen.

Looking back up into the bronze face of Daniele Manin, Marco spoke to his new, old friend. "I will tell the people, Manin. I will shout it. I will foam like a prophet. I will write about it and force the people to hear me. Even if they laugh, they will know. Their grandfathers will remember, and they too will spread the word!"

He collapsed there and cried for several minutes. When he'd regained composure, he headed home.

CHAPTER 22

THE MEANING OF DYING

"That's quite the story, Marco," his father said over a shared espresso. "It also seems a fantastical stretch to explain the decline of Venice. It is much like the stories our grandfathers would tell us to make us behave when I was a child, only this one I had never heard. I hope you don't expect people to believe it's real. Perhaps you should write an article about this but focus on the lack of responsibility and the lack of care, not on the stories of magic and a dying city."

Marco had awakened with the extraordinary energy that morning. He was not going to let his father's doubts destroy his motivation. He left for school and went straight to the mayor's office. Marco and the mayor had gotten to know each other since Marco had started school there. The mayor had been a professor of philosophy long before taking office. He appreciated Marco's personality.

"Hello this is Marco, Stephanie, how you are doing?" he said to the mayor's secretary. "Is the mayor available to come to the phone for a second?"

"Let me check," she said. "One moment."

"Hello, Marco what is going on?"

"Mr. Mayor, did you have your coffee yet? How about a coffee at Rosa Salva in Campo San Luca?"

"Sure," the mayor said. "I have a little break in an hour. We can meet then."

———

As they sipped their coffee, Marco began, hesitantly at first.

"I am here to request your help. I believe that Venice is in danger of dying. I believe that if we do not motivate the people to love our city like they once did, it will give up and crumble into the ocean. I want to get people to love Venice again, to take pride in her, to take care of her. Can this be done?"

The mayor responded, "I do not know, Marco. I am aware of Venice's current plight, but I cannot guarantee that we will be able to fix it."

Marco sipped thoughtfully, allowing the expectant pause to add dramatics to the conversation. "I am concerned. Nobody wants to die. Why does Venice have to? For ages, people have tried to find a reason not to die. Some have spent all their life just trying to justify their deaths, trying to believe that they are benefitting when they die, but still who wants to die? I don't believe in deathism. I don't believe that just because death is inevitable and inescapable that it must be accepted as a positive thing. I think we all ought to be incredibly sad and depressed about this absolute fact of life, and we should be angry for it, for we only have days left until the inevitable end comes when all my angst dissolves into nothing."

"Don't fall in this ancient trap of obsessing over death. You'll find yourself in the embalming game like the Egyptians." The mayor chuckled over the rim of his cup.

"No!" Marco said, suddenly aware that he'd raised his voice and calming his tone. "I understand what you are saying, sir, but that is not what I mean at all. Venice will *disappear*. It will become a thing of legend to our grandchildren. It will no longer have a place on the maps of the earth. It will be as Atlantis and Lemuria, merely tall tales for children to be fascinated by. Where in the world you can find canals bridges, small calles, campiellos, a quiet walk into the history of humanity with churches from different religions, with paintings by world-famous painters? The smell of the lagoon the sun reflecting on the old building, the magic of the morning mist, the mystery of the winter fogs."

"I don't understand what exactly it is that you want me to do."

"I believe we can stop this," Marco said evenly. "But I won't accept spiritual survival as an excuse to allow Venice to die right in front of me."

"You know," said the mayor, "the Muslims believe that this physical life is not the true life. The entire lifetime of a Muslim is a chain of trials and tests by which his final destiny is determined. For him, death is the return of the soul to Allah. If he behaves correctly, then he will be rewarded in Heaven when he meets Allah. Ergo, the inevitability of death is never far from his awareness. This helps him to keep all his life and deeds in perspective as he tries to live in preparedness for what is to come."

"Do you believe that?"

The mayor smiled. "As an atheist, I wish to remain agnostic on the matter."

"I am serious, sir."

"And so am I, Marco. Our culture is a Catholic culture. We are taught to believe that our body is just as integral to our personhood as the soul. When Christ comes again, our bodies will resurrect and join our souls. For Christianity, body and soul are one and connected even if at death the soul is separated from the body and so the body decomposes as the immortal soul returns to God, blah blah blah. Come, I think the smell of burnt coffee is polluting our thoughts. Let's walk."

CHAPTER 23

THE MEANING OF HELL

Marco and the mayor remained silent as they walked side by side toward San Marco square.

"Your namesake, no?"

"Would you believe I never asked?"

The mayor threw his head back in a laugh. "You of all people!"

"I wish to hear more of your thoughts."

"I'm getting to them. It is quite an interesting concept that nobody nowadays really seems to care about purgatory, paradise, and hell. They all think they will go to paradise. It seems they all deserve to go to paradise. I once had a student in class who said he deserved an A on his test, when he tested with an F! They don't study they don't make any effort, and they think the society will take care of them just because they exist! Come with me I want you to meet someone."

They entered the Cathedral of St. Mark from a small door on the side instead of the main entrance, where there was a long line.

"This is a majestic church," said the mayor. "But you do realize, don't you, that this church was really built to show off the opulence of Venice in the 11th century. The mosaic, the richness of the church, created a nickname.

"*La Chiesa d'oro*," said a priest coming out from one of the confessionals. "The gold church for the pride of the Venetian."

"Hello, Monsignor Luciani," said the mayor shaking his hand. "How are you? This is Marco, a good friend of mine."

"Hello, Monsignor," said Marco. "It is an honor to meet you in person. I always enjoy your Sunday homily."

"And you are here to convert our mutual friend?" the priest said, gesturing to the mayor and shooting the man a wink.

"I am trying to convert him on other matters at present."

"Marco is trying to save Venice," said the mayor.

"Ah, well, you'll need more than religion to do that, I'm afraid."

"So we've been discussing," said the mayor.

Marco noticed how thin and small in stature this priest was. He had white hair and wore a pair of glasses so large they nearly took over his kind face.

"Then might I ask, what was the purpose of your visit here?" Luciani asked this very calmly, as if he had been in the process of receiving both the mayor and Marco for confession.

"What if there was a curse?" asked Marco. "A curse that dooms you to failure. A curse that no matter how hard you try to escape it, guarantees you a lifetime of suffering. Do you think such a curse exists?"

"Hmm," Luciani answered. "Are we discussing a curse from God?"

Marco stared for a moment. "Say, for argument's sake, that is the case."

"Well then, first, I think we need to decide whether such a curse would be unfair or not. In the case of being issued from God the Father, then yes, it would be fair and just. And now I ask you, do the wicked not deserve to be punished?"

"Yes" said Marco, flustered. "Of course they do, but—"

"Yes," said Luciani, "Christian teaching has always maintained that the wicked are doomed to spend an eternity in hell."

Luciani was still talking, but Marco's attention was taken elsewhere. From the apse towards the entrance, items inside the painting appeared to be moving. It was the history of salvation, with the prophets, the ascension, and the Pentecost. The saints were moving fast, leaving the heart to go to the promised heaven as they were afraid to stay on heart one minute more. He shivered. He looked at the dome. A voice floated there like a cloud.

Marco, Heaven does exist. Work on it and you will be there with us.

Marco recognized the voices of St. John and St Leonard, speaking where they were located over the transept, in the dome of the church. They were moving to different scenes of St. John the Evangelist's life, and they shifted from their painting to the domes to show Marco a scene from the life of Christ. Marco found he could not move.

Luciani and the mayor were walking towards the refectory, and when they realized that Marco was left behind, they came back to him. They noticed he was looking at the dome painting.

"I'm sure that even the most evil of men did one or two good things in their lives," said Marco. "The only way for someone to deserve eternal punishment is for every single one of his actions to be irredeemably evil. And to think that one can be the incarnation of Satan from the moment that one leaves the womb is hard to fathom. We are incapable of infinite acts, and so we should not be slapped with infinite punishment. That is why, with the blessing of the Lord, we can be safe and still reach Paradise."

Luciani turned his head away from Marco and looked off to the side. His gaze was directed at a bookshelf standing along the wall of the refectory, but he was looking at something else, something that was not there, as if the image before his eyes was one that came from his mind, or perhaps his memory.

"Sister Mary," interrupted Luciani, "it is always good to see you. This is the mayor Ongaro, and this is Marco. Don't you have those beautiful cookies you and your sister usually make? I'd like to offer them to our guests?"

"Yes, Father, I will get some." The sister disappeared for a few minutes.

Ongaro focused his gaze on Marco. "You think everyone is so innocent? You think that if Hell existed that there would be no one that would deserve to go there? Marco, by your same logic, there would be no one who deserves to go to Heaven, either. If humans are incapable of *eternal* acts, as you might say, and thus do not deserve eternal consequences, then no human can deserve eternal happiness either—because we are incapable of doing something infinitely good. I don't believe that anyone comes out of the womb as righteous as God Himself, either."

Marco was surprised at the mayor's new tone of voice. "Well, isn't that what purgatory is for?"

"Yes," replied the priest. "It gives us a chance to redeem ourselves. We suffer in purgatory, but not forever. I suppose that in theory, all people can suffer according to the severity of their crimes. But the Protestants contemptuously deny the idea of Purgatory and fervently insist upon Hell. They believe that some people are destined for eternal reward and others for eternal punishment."

Sister Mary returned bearing a tray. "You know, my monsignor, that these, with a little of your wine..." She cleared her throat and smiled.

"Ah! How could I have been so forgetful," said Luciani, making his way toward the small shelves on the back of the room. He came back with three small glasses and a bottle of the wine. He served the two men.

"Is this sacramental wine?" asked Marco.

"It has not been consecrated, if that's what you mean."

"Precisely," said Marco, proceeding then to dunk the hard cookie in the richly dark wine.

"It is always amazing to me," said Ongaro, "how can you have this aromatic wine. It definitely stands among all I am trying to do," said the mayor.

"Yes," added Marco, "this wine! This cookie! *This* is heaven."

"Going back to our discussion," added Luciani. "They say that there is no act that we are capable of which can change our fate. That is entirely up to God. Me, I believe that there are those who are born with good hearts and those who are evil to their core. The Lord shows us that we can purify even the evil."

Ongaro frowned. "You cannot unscramble eggs and you cannot wash away sin. Those who are evil are going to remain evil, and, if I believed in God, I think He ought to punish them. However, I do believe that the world has a natural way of punishing the wicked."

Marco looked down dejectedly. "Do you think Venice is being punished for her crimes? Do you think that she can't wash away her sins? Maybe she deserves the fate that will befall her. She is being punished by proxy for our apathy."

The mayor appeared startled by Marco's response. "No—no Marco," he began, "you keep coming back to this. I don't believe Venice is doomed."

"Can we shift the hell-bound obsession we have for our possessions, to a divine passion for the city we live in?"

Luciani looked a little puzzled.

"Monsignor," the mayor said, "Marco has been telling me that Venice is doomed and there is a spell that will take Venice out of this world since the Venetian did not take care of it."

Luciani stared, abashed.

Marco said, "Venice is dirty with pungent odors, scratched and cracked buildings, and total apathy from the people. She is a leper, condemned to be this way by the sins of her fathers. What can we do? Nothing? Watch the dying of Venice and bemoan her fate? We're living through a very personal descent into Hell that Dante could illustrate for us, and we act as if there is nothing to be done about it. We're not even taking the high tides seriously, and even school children know that danger."

"Yes, Marco," Ongaro said, seeming suddenly tired. "You are right. But there is so very little that we can do. Nobody does anything, but everyone seeks credit. There is no government money to bail us out this time. I know that Venice is in a decadent state."

Marco was breathing hard, and his knuckles were white from how hard he was gripping his chair. He thought the mayor may have noticed that and wanted to calm down the situation. "Let's leave this conversation open. We can meet tomorrow if you like and leave the monsignor to his job to save souls. Would you meet me at the cafe tomorrow? We'll have coffee and discuss this more. We need to ask the help of the central government and bypass the local petty political maneuvering. We must approach a more powerful resource."

Luciani then said, "Marco, God has a plan and sometimes we do not know what it is and why it is one way or the other. I am not sure about Venice disappearing, but I do agree about the decadence of the city. Even in the church during the Mass, people are more focused on their earthly issues. They check their texts and email. Several times during the Mass, I lose my concentration by looking at so many people talking amongst themselves instead of to God." He took a little breath and blessed them in his heart. *"Father, forgive them, for they know not what they do."* He then continued. "You know, many people say they believe they are following a religion, but many of those say it more like a cliché, the same way they say they have a nice house, nice car, etc. They show off their religion without really believing in it. So they come to church as they go to work as a duty, and not as fulfillment. These people don't believe. They will never know the difference between eternal life or faith. At this time, the best description of faith and the eternal life or punishment comes from people who are not religious at all. The best example is Dante. I don't know how much he believed in and how much he wanted to go to church. Even if in those times, if you were not going to church, everybody noticed. But he made a great description of the other life that still many people follow or believe, sometimes more than the one indicated by God."

"I have to go back to my office," the mayor said. "I am quite late. Thank you, Monsignor for your time. Marco, I will see you tomorrow at 11."

Marco thanked Luciani, who gave the young man a fatherly hug before departing.

"Marco, would you like for me to hear your confession?"

"I think you may just have, Father."

The old priest smiled and blessed his forehead.

———

"Marco," said Ongaro after several minutes walking in silence, "tomorrow there is a demonstration which will travel from Piazzale Roma to Piazza San Marco. There will be speakers. Would you go and talk about Venice?"

Marco stopped and turned to face the man. "You're serious."

"Deadly serious."

"Of course," he said, shaking his head as from disbelief. "Thank you. Thank you!"

———

Marco was close to home, but he did not want to head there yet. His head was still swimming with the prospect of speaking at the demonstration.

The square was still full of people watching, taking pictures, and playing with the pigeons. The middle of the square was empty, so Marco headed there. He faced the cathedral, so beautiful with the sunlight reflecting the ancient splendor. The tower of Venice was there standing strong on the right side and the two Mores statues still ready to hit the bells at every hour as they did for hundreds of years, on the left. Right below the Quadri café, two guitarists played Bach. On the opposite side under the porticoes that wrapped all around the building in the square was the Florian Caffe, probably the most famous of all the old cafes in Venice—a baroque pearl. There, facing the cathedral, stood the Museum Correr. The pigeons were flying everywhere, children were playing and running as Marco did when he himself was the terror of all pigeons. He was certain they recognized him, since they flew away as soon as his shadow appeared, hovering over them.

Those childhood times were good times, he thought, painfully aware that now, as a grown man, he could no longer run freely without problems as he once did. He could not stop bringing his thoughts back to what the monsignor had said moments earlier. The words of Dante had come up in their conversation. Thoughts of Dante made him think about nothing other than the mystery girl behind the book he had found at the museum.

Where is she? What is she doing? Marco asked himself. *When will I meet her to declare my love for her?* He had begun to love her in his heart without even knowing her. Yet, maybe she was actually Fata Morgana who had become human in order to take him away from all this pain and sorrow.

"Morgana where are you?" he asked aloud to anyone who would listen. "Is it you?"

Why then would Morgana write *Leifde*, a Dutch word? He could have read the words, Love, Amor, Habibi, or other forms.

No, wait a minute, not possible. She would be from the Netherlands, maybe from Amsterdam, the so-called Venice of the north.

She would understand canals and boats.

She would be perfect.

CHAPTER 24

INVOLVING THE CITIZENS

After a good night's sleep, early in the morning, he went to Piazzale Roma. Banners of all kinds called for a better Venice for the people, or for people to be better to Venice. Politicians, celebrities, and working people marched side-by-side with Venice's finest academics.

Marco was the first to take the stage and address the people in the Piazza. There, in the crowd, he saw the apparition of Cicero, stern and bald-headed. Cicero's countenance then changed, and he gave Marco a wink.

"Ladies and gentlemen," Marco began, "thank you for caring enough to be here today, for loving our fair city, and for doing what each of you can to make a difference. We have inherited Venice from our forefathers, and she is as a city lives and breathes. She needs people to care for her. For too long now we have stood by and let people befoul her body, littering her streets, urinating in her canals. The City of Water has become a harlot, stinking of our degradation. Her stench permeates our nostrils as we eat."

He paused to receive a smattering of applause punctuated by whistles.

"Now," he continued, I have heard your complaints, though they beat as softly as hearts. But like hearts, they will pump the lifeblood back into

Venice. I know you cannot take it anymore. Every day in your campiellos you have to remove the trash and the cat food and excrement. The real owners of Venice are our cats, scrounging food from our trash bags while the rats multiply and grow as big as cats themselves. Pigeons contaminate our fountains and our statuary. Do we clean the statues? Do we do anything at all to decrease the number of pigeons, rats, and feral cats in Venice?

"I hear your heartbeats, friends. I know that every time you turn into some hidden calle, the odor of urine is impossible to take. Are there not enough public bathrooms in Venice? We have stood by while our calles became toilets. I hear your heartbeats. I hear you lamenting how the canals have not be cleaned. I hear your fears of acid in the filthy water eating right through your basements. Either we sit down at the table and structure a plan to clean, save, and maintain our home, or we abandon her to nature one Piazza at a time!"

Another round of applause, more fervent this time, rose from the crowd. Cicero had disappeared from his spot in the audience and was nowhere to be found. Marco assumed the soul of the great man must have entered his body. There was no other explanation.

"In the past, the city would completely block the canals and clean the bottoms of them, and not just with some giant vacuum. The problem, my friends, is a mirror of Venice's structure. At her heart is accumulated dirt and sludge. She must be purged of it. Even the little that we do is not done well. We see Venice every day, and the change has come about slowly, but now the change requires attention, or we are in trouble. The calle and the campielli are vandalized, littered, and filthy. My fellow Venetians, we deserve better, but it requires us to do the work, to find our sense of civic duty and care for her. Our children will inherit what we leave them. Venice should live forever. We must be committed to her preservation."

The crowd applauded again, with cried echoing his last words.

"But it all starts with us," said Marco. "If you throw trash in the calles and the canals without thinking, start thinking and stop throwing. If you see tourists throwing trash in the streets and the waterways, tell them to stop and to pick it up. We are losing tourist dollars due to the filth spread by irresponsible people who both live and visit here. We do not need any more lecturers, we need vigilantes!

"You may remember that people used to swim in the Grand Canal. Nobody would dare to do that now. Venice was the Most Serene Republic. How is it possible that the canals could be cleaned regularly over 800 years ago, but it costs too much today? What are we going to leave our children? Our beautiful city that is like no other in the world needs us, and our legacy to our grandchildren depends upon us. It is time to police ourselves. It is time to stop tourists and others from adding to the filth that is already plaguing our city. It is time to make our politicians and leaders listen to us until they restructure the way Venice is run until we can all keep her clean. If we don't do this, nobody will."

The applause that followed Marco's oratory was lengthy and passionate. The people who had gathered there felt the weight of his words. The city was theirs to care for, the legacy marked for their children.

The day after Marco had spoken publicly, the local newspaper ran a front-page article with his name and picture like some returning Olympian. There were the obvious calls for a new city manager, with an embedded hint that Marco could be the one.

At lunchtime, he saw men and women who sitting at cafe tables sipping wine, talking about the fiery young man who would save Venice, all while ignoring papers blowing down the Calle, stuffing their noses with their own exhalations to disguise the smells.

He tried to remain in his own glory, remembering the sounds of adulation. His pride was checked, however, when he thought of his Venice, his love, defiled as she was. And the pride he took now was in the idea that *perhaps he had indeed been heard.*

His thoughts went back to the book he had found the day before, which he carried with him in his backpack. He decided then to walk again to St. Mark Square.

Once inside the museum, he stopped by the front desk. A clerk sat there looking officious and stiff.

"Was anybody looking for a book? *La Vita Nova*?"

"What is that title again?"

He gave it to her, spelling it out. This new generation of Italians were ignorant about their origin, their ancestors, their history, and about the important books which made the Italian language. He left without hope.

He would hold on to the book. Asking any more about it would be too painful for him. It was Zeno's paradox of the arrow. He would never catch the owner, for she would be ahead of him for eternity. He had to settle for the fact that if it was his destiny to meet this person, then one day he would.

Later that evening, after supper, Marco read a few pages of the book, and again he fell asleep holding it like a lover.

CHAPTER 25

THE LIFE IN VENICE

In the days that followed, Marco found that he had a sort of super-power. Everywhere he went, if someone was about to throw litter on the ground in his presence, they would see him, hesitate, and then take that litter to the nearest trash bin. Most had the decency to look down with shame as they did so, and then would walk away looking defiantly proud. It amused Marco, but it gave him no hope. The government, of course, did nothing. Their lack of action and limited response was part of an ancient Italian tradition.

—

During that summer, Marco lived the life of a Venetian with his friends, haunting the bacari around Venice for cicchetti and ombra and glasses of Santa Maria Formosa wine. They spoke of Rome—Giorgio's father worked for an import and export company and often found himself in Rome with his wily son in tow. And they spoke of architecture and history. And they marveled at the delicacies—polpette and the polenta and baccala, and the wines one could only find in that region, in the heart of his city, his love.

One night he and Giorgio ended up spending hours together talking and laughing. It was a relief for Marco, who tended to let the weight of the world and its woes weigh heavily on his shoulders.

They made plans to convene in Lido for a poker game with friends, losing their shirts while bathing in the scent of the Adriatic.

Marco was elated when he found himself fifty euros richer at four in the morning with four queens as his benefactors.

And they camped on the beach and fed their fires through the night, enjoying modern jazz and the company of one another. And the Raboso was excellent. And there were jokes at Marco's expense. And there was the sun rising.

In the mist of the new light, Marco saw a figure rising up from the sea. It was a woman walking with an old man. The man had a black pointed hat and a long beard. She had dark hair with a long vest on top of her dress. They were arguing. He jumped up and went close to the water get a better look. Alas, the strengthening sun deleted the vision from the water and the sky took its place.

It was time to leave. They collected their things, and together they walked from the beach to the main street in Lido. Viale Santa Maria Elizabetta was still empty. There was one garbage truck collecting the trash. Another truck was cleaning the road. And the aromas of fresh croissants began to fill the air.

"Today will be a great day," said Marco. The wind teasing the lagoon, the smell of fresh water, and the sunrise remained inside of him.

Marco bought the Sunday edition of the *Gazzettino* for his father to read while the old man sipped his coffee.

"Well," said his father, "if it isn't the prodigal son and his shadow. Long night, eh?" He gave a chuckle. "Don't worry, when I was young, I would go to parties on Saturday and then to work on Sunday morning, then afterwards go right to the soccer game at San Helen. That's when the Venice team was actually good. Now we're in the third division and it's embarrassing. The kitchen is yours. Don't wake up your mother. Oh, and thanks for the newspaper." He waved with the *Gazzettino* and retired to his chair to snore away his Sunday.

———

Giorgio spent the night in deep sleep but in the morning was ready to join Marco at the Zattere a the long stretch in the canal del la Giudecca opposite to the Mulino Stucchi. From there they could see the boats delivering hordes of tourists to Venice. They streamed of the boats with their cameras, hats, mosquito spray bottles, with sunscreen slathered on their noses and foreheads. And they walked like downtrodden, taking tentative steps as if they feared their collective weight might sink the city.

"Don't you think that this town is magic?" said Marco.

Giorgio made no effort to hide his eyeroll. "Why do I sense another rousing speech?"

"You will not deflate me this time, my friend. Look at this. The water here has a different smell. I guess since the Canal de La Giudecca is deeper and larger, it smells like the ocean, and then when you look up, you see another island, la Giudecca just in front of us. How could man, more than a thousand years ago, build such a beauty?"

"You're putting me in the mood to fill myself with the beauty of Venice. It's one of the occupational hazards of having you as a friend. You realize that, don't you?"

Marco smiled. "It's the hidden places that are the best. Only there you can see the true Venice without the ravages of time. But despite all the merry-making of the past couple of days, I still feel like a man wandering alone through a desert. There has never been a time when I haven't felt lonely. I could be sitting around a fire on the beach at Lido, singing and laughing with our friends, and yet I found myself more than once staring into the fire in prayerful meditation, asking for help to save this beautiful city. I can't shake this sense of dread. It's like a sickness in me that goes dormant for small stretches of time, then wakes. But it's always there."

"I hate it when you get in that mood," said Giorgio. "There is nothing I can do to make it better. I remember one time Tiziano was with us, and he tried to cheer you out of your melancholy only to have you tear into him with a passionate tirade about the impending death of Venice."

Marco waved a hand. "Don't remind me."

"For over an hour you lectured the poor guy, tears of passion and frustration running down your cheeks. It's maddening to watch, and pure hell to be on the receiving end of it."

"I know," said Marco, fingering the slats of the bench they shared. "And the worst part is that after I've sunk into one of those pits of despair, I just leave and go home. I know I am not good company anymore at that point. I don't even want to be around myself but I'm stuck with me. Can I tell you something?"

"If you're going to commit suicide, I'd rather it be a surprise," said Giorgio.

"I'm serious. It was during one of those journeys home after blowing up at a friend, when I was walking the calles and crossing the bridges, I let myself accept that nobody cared about Venice as I do. It wasn't self-pity, I told myself. It was the truth. Nobody cared enough to clean the city or to maintain her anymore. Now, I'll tell you a secret, Giorgio. I have often imagined Daniele Manin, Merlin, Morgan le Fay, and all the other heroes of Venetian legend looking down on me and on us with disappointment and looking down on the rest of Venice with disdain."

"You were born with too much passion, if you don't mind my saying. You can become one of the Paladins of Venice, and a good one, at that. Don't despair!" He shook his head. "The only thing you have to fear is your descent into premature old age." He started to laugh, and his friend got caught up in it.

"I feel like an old man," said Marco. "You know, I often wonder if Venetians have to have a plague or some disaster to wake up them up before they realize their weakness. I mean, they built the Madonna Della Salute to thank the Virgin for saving them from the Black Death."

He paused, then added. "Maybe next time will be too late."

———

The trip home did him little good, as they'd passed through litter and graffiti spoiled streets.

Marco's parents had gone to visit his father's brother in Mestre, so Marco knew they would not be home until late that evening. Home alone, he found some eggplant parmigiana in the fridge. Afterwards, he found that he was exhausted much earlier than usual. The sun hadn't set yet.

He heard a voice on the breeze. Captivated, stirred, he sank into it.

When he started awake, night had settled completely. In this hazy dark, he wondered whether what he saw in Lido was a mirage of Fata Morgana. And he wondered if Fata Morgana had indeed chosen to live in Sicily. Was she not supposed to be in Venice? He had the same question about the mystery girl who owned the book. Wasn't she also supposed to be in Venice?

He remembered that Beatrice not only led Dante through Hell but also cleaned his face of the stains. It was a thought that took hold of him until he slept.

CHAPTER 26

THE PROFESSOR CRICKET AND A CIVIC SENSE

As Marco made his way to the kitchen for his first cup of coffee the next morning, he felt a detached sensation, one that came on from time to time like depression or a bout of allergies. And on its heels, the lingering notion that time was running out.

He remembered a professor he had met at a conference. "Cricket"—the name derived from the man's habit of chirping nasally whenever he suppressed a sneeze—was a scholar of Latin and Greek. He had once told Marco that he enjoyed teaching high school because "college involved too much politics and bureaucracy." He had no time for it, and preferred spending his energy fully immersed in Seneca or Cicero. Cricket lived in the Mestre district, a mainland part of the city where many Venetians had migrated to over the years in search of work and homes. Cricket's house was open to anyone who would care to debate on different subjects about Italy, its literature, and its history. Students from both the high school and university sat for hours on the rug in his living room debating, recharging their philosophical batteries, and broadening their world views. It was a symposium without the wine.

Marco rang the bell at Cricket's front door. Cricket answered in his robe, his beard wildly unkempt as it always was.

"Well," he said, expelling a perfume of coffee from his mouth, "if it isn't the mayor of Venice! Welcome, Your Honor! Come in, come in!"

Marco stepped into the man's simple home, remembering the scents of those afternoons steeped in debate. He looked around as if trying to find a ghost of himself hiding somewhere in one of the corners.

"You look troubled," said Cricket, closing the door softly.

Marco turned to him. "It's because I am."

"Can I get you some coffee?"

"Please."

Cricket busied himself at a Chemex and an electric gooseneck kettle speaking with flourishes as he worked. "Normally I would begin with simple pleasantries. And perhaps you'd ask me about the coffee I'm serving you. Or else I'd offer the information without your having to ask. But, as it stands, it seems there is a more pressing matter. Tell me, please, what has emptied your heart on this beautiful morning?"

Marco told Cricket about his dreams. Cricket inhaled deeply.

"Shortly after we met," Cricket told his friend, "you brought me a poem that made me worry about you for quite some time. Do you remember it?"

"I do."

Cricket removed the gently boiling kettle from its cradle and began pouring water over the grounds in concentric circles. "I would be delighted if you would recite it to me."

Marco stared down at his shoes for a moment, then began:

"Always sadness in his words,
Ignorant of happiness.
In this short life without a 'why,'
Happiness does not last,
But sadness is immeasurable.
And so it will be until the day where water will wash every-
thing away
Like the rains in May."

Cricket sat and listened respectfully, and when the poem ended, he looked his young friend in the eye and told him, "I've learned since then that you are far more resilient than that sad poem implies. You know that about yourself, too, but sometimes you forget it, or don't let yourself believe it. I think this is one of those times."

"Perhaps you're right."

"Let's drink our coffee and speak of fun things, eh? I'm expecting some students in a short while. I insist you stick around and join in whatever debate ensues. Would you do that for me? Indulge an old man in his penchant for poisoning the minds of youths?"

Marco smiled. "I would consider it an honor."

———

Six students of varying ages arrived one by one. They began with pleasantries, as Cricket had implied was his want to do. And shortly, a debate ensued over civic duty and a utopian society.

When the time was right, Marco felt it was time to add his views.

"I think problems arise because people lack the care needed to remedy them. And so, we get caught in a loop. We are disgusted by dirt and grime, we say it is unacceptable, and yet we put up with it, and we accuse everybody else of causing the problem. Meanwhile, we continue adding to the filth, oblivious of our contradictions. Notice the walls of our city have become a public place for graffiti—pornographic literature free to the public! And no one wants to take responsibility. I feel disgusted when I look around the city. Where is the moral obligation?

A young student with a failed attempt at a beard began to speak, but Marco held a hand up.

"A moment please," he said. "There's more. I am upset with the people of the city. They seem to believe they are entitled to have things they had not worked for and therefore do not deserve. How could they have anything they did not work for? Material things require work! Relationships require work, no?"

"One of the biggest problems with modern relationships," said Cricket, rising to walk among his students like a sage, "*is precisely* the sense of entitlement. People think they are entitled to what they want without regard for the work it takes to make it. So, I agree with you, Marco. But, you see, they consider the work to be someone else's problem and not theirs. Where does such a mindset originate?"

"We overwhelm each other just by existing," concluded Marco.

"That is a thought, Marco." said Cricket. "And so, perhaps a sense of civic duty is necessary for the creation of a utopian society, but with a natural aversion to civic duty, is utopia possible? If we stick with the dictionary definition of a utopian society, we will be discussing the problem until Santoro here grows his beard."

They students enjoyed a hearty laugh at the young man's expense.

"My beard is thin, but it's an educated one," he countered.

The afternoon continued with the conversation running the gamut from More to Marx to Nietzsche. It was a balm to Marco's weary soul, and a rigorous workout of his intellect. When they agreed to discontinue the debate, they went out for aperitifs of white wine and Aperol. From there they each went to their respective homes for the night.

Marco had needed this day to recharge.

Creating the perfect society would have to wait until another day.

CHAPTER 27

WALKING THROUGH VENICE

He awoke the next morning listening to his thoughts, knowing that the sour mood he was nurturing would not do him any good. He wondered what the mystery woman looked like as he reached under his pillow, found the book, and held it in his hand, touching the outside leather binding, running his finger down the spine, smelling the intoxicating aroma from the leather. He yearned to find her. Then thumbing through the pages, he read her notes, pausing only to turn back to previous pages, reading again and again. He stopped and forced himself to focus his mind back on his journey. Marco put the book under his pillow again for safekeeping, dressed casually for the day, slipping into a comfortable linen shirt. He took a deep breath and walked outside the house, allowing the beautiful sky and endless horizon to help bolster his mood. Marco enjoyed taking the back roads of Venice, those that tourists only found by accident. If only the owner of his mystery book would show up to comfort him, he would tell her everything, and he knew without a doubt that she would understand him. He tried to conjure her out of air but found he could only come up with partial features. A dark, luminous eye, an arched brow, full lips, hair flowing around her shoulders. Back to work, he thought. Shake it off.

The Fondamente Della Misericordia was one of Marco's favorite routes. He carried food and coats to donate to the less fortunate as part of his usual social service work, but he felt uneasy because of the previous day's riot. He didn't stop to chit chat with some of his college friends he met along the way, who already filled up the slot at the few Bacari on the route. All he could think about was how life seemed to ebb and flow without reason. But his disgust in seeing more graffiti and smelling urine every time he walked down a small calle or turned a corner, made his rage grow.

"Venice in serie A," read one graffiti. *"Juve merda: Viva Inter,"* was another phrase. *Why did people feel the need to write about soccer on an ancient wall? Why the desire to mar history?* Another one scrawled, "Marcella always in my heart," someone pouring out his heart. Marco understood the need for love, but why not just send a card or an email, instead of spreading his heart all over a wall?

Marco always liked the quieter areas of Venice that tourists rarely saw. Yes, everybody wants to see the Rialto Bridge and Saint Mark's Square, but Marco always knew that there was so much more to Venice. He liked to stand at the end of the St. Helena area, at the point facing the island of Lido, which had been protecting the lagoon from the turmoil of the sea and aquatic invasions. It was a thin, long tongue of land with two small openings for the sea to mix with the lagoon at its northernmost and southernmost points. In St. Helena, there was a beautiful park and a hidden soccer stadium that a person could find only if looking hard. At St. Helena, nature could speak to a person if he was willing to listen. There, one could find serenity.

Walking back from St. Helena towards Saint Mark's square, Marco passed by the Calle Della Misericordia. "Run, shoot, defense." He could still hear those voices when he went there to watch basketball games. The Basket Reyer was in the first division. The team was doing so well that the city built the Basketball Arena, but right before that, there arose one of the pearls of Venice that Marco knew would be soon forgotten—the Arsenale.

Marco stood at the place where Venetians built their boats and ships, acclaimed throughout the world. They were the pride of Venice, once seen sailing all across the seas. Now they just made gondolas for the enchantment of tourists. "It is a beauty," Marco said to a worker busy filling in the wood of a gondola in the making. "It must take a lot of time to complete one," he said, seeing a wooden body without the classical black color.

"It is," said the man in his middle sixties, with a face burned by the sea. "The real Gondola takes time." Marco could see the love the man put into his work, paying attention to details, and conducting multiple tweaks to make the boat perfect. "Now the people like to buy from the Chinese or from corporations! Don't let me talk about it," he said angrily. "They take away the jobs from us and they make Gondolas that will sink with the first wave. They are ruining the artisan jobs but also the good name of this famous Venetian boat-building business." He sighed.

"I sympathize with you," replied Marco. "Everything is replaced with low-quality material that does not even look Venetian at all. "

Marco shook his head sadly, said good-bye, and left.

Going from the back calles, Marco imagined himself as a tourist and saw it again through a foreigner's eyes. One could get to San Mark square passing by quiet campi and campielli that speak to the privacy, the beauty, the serenity of Venice.

Marco found himself then in the Calle dei Fuseri, then in the Frezzaria. He felt at home in the Frezzaria with its calles, piscina, and bridge. It was in the Frezzaria where arrows used to be made. The surname "Frezza" might have meant arrow maker in the past, but not now. While there was no longer the call for arrows from Venice, the artisanal qualities of the area remained. Marco knew that some Frezzas were found in the south of Italy and had been pirates. He didn't care if it was the same people. The Frezzaria felt comfortable and like a second home to him. His dad told him that his great-grandmother was living in Calle dei Fabbri, and they had kept a house there for generations. Unfortunately, his uncle had sold it when she passed. Such a shame. He walked on to Campo San Fantin and to the Ateneo Veneto where the Venetian region's culture was preserved.

Marco's thoughts wandered to Venice's grand history. His beloved city had been around for many years and had many stories to tell, from defending itself against Attila the Hun, to fighting for its independence. He thought back on that history and brought it up in the forefront of his mind. He imagined he was telling the history to a group of tourists, and he could almost hear his voice resonating in pride to the group.

"For many centuries, you know, Italy had had four great maritime republics: Venice, Genova, Amalfi, and Pisa. From the 10th to the 13th centuries, they built fleets of ships both for their protection and to support extensive trade networks across the Mediterranean, giving them an essential role in the Crusades. They were not monarchies, but real republics. Venice and Genova were strongholds, and the two cities fought for control of the Mediterranean. It was said that Marco Polo, the Venetian who discovered China, was a prisoner in Genova and was caught during one of the wars, then left to die there. Just those stories can fill up an entire museum with memories and papers. Venice was also a model of the republic with two, and not just one, president that they called doges. They have a kind of a parliament and democratic decision-making process. I know that today it might not sound like much, but in 1,000 AD, that was an innovative idea. So much history there that you could not even begin to fathom it.

Marco recalled from some of his favorite history classes that the richness of Venice came from the trades. You could find almost anything in 1,200 ADE, spices, clothes, pearls. At the time it seemed that people did not understand how history went and how much Venice had lost over the years—power, wealth, and much more.

Marco could spend hours walking around Venice. Sometimes he wished he could be a tour guide. He knew Venice so well that he could give a history lesson on any part of the city. He was always impressed by how many gondolas could work during the day. Il Ponte dei fuseri was his favorite place. The fuseri were families that used to melt and mold elements like copper and iron. The bridge was constructed in 1755, located within sestiere San Marco, crossing the Rio dei Fuseri. It was a single-arch type of bridge with a metal railing, a great place for photos of the Ponte de Le Colonne and Gondolas.

Marco started to imagine himself as a tour guide: "Ladies and gentlemen, please follow me to St. Mark's Square. The most famous sestiere in Venice has one of the world's most famous squares, St. Mark's. Anchored on one end by the basilica, clustered around it are restaurants, museums, shops, orchestras playing in the square, pigeons, the grand pink doge's Palace or Palazzo Ducale, the soaring campanile bell tower, an astrological clock tower, plus gorgeous cafes and restaurants like Florian and Quadri. Piazza San Marco is beloved by Venetians themselves. They book a table anytime, which offers a buffer from the fray. This grand outdoor drawing room attracts Venetians for a stroll, too, especially late in the afternoon when the hordes of day trippers thin out."

He was proud of himself, finding a job during the summer. He imagined people asking questions, specifically of the two big statues that for centuries have been hitting a bell at the hour mark. The statues of three Moors, plus their servant, seem to come alive from the walls of the buildings. Originally, the statues were modeled after the legend of the Mori. There were three brothers from Morea/Peloponnese—Sandi, Afani and Rioba Mastelli. Silk and spice merchants, they moved to Venice in 1112, where they built Palazzo Mastelli as the seat of their business. The Mastelli

Brothers were notorious for their shady dealings and eager participation in doge Dondolo's sacking of Constantinople. The legend goes that the three brothers were turned to stone because of their greed. Another legend says Maria Magdalena herself turned them into stone for their hard-hearted business dealings. This is a quiet and evocative little corner of Venice, particularly in the evening.

Marco gazed at the Moors, at the Museo Correr, right next to the calle that went to the opera house just around the corner. After taking a short look at the next exhibit, he stopped in the campo in front of the opera house. He remembered a night when he had walked past Il Teatro La Fenice to watch the people coming out of the theater after the Opera. The finery they were dressed in, the opulence of it, all added to the air they projected, making Marco wonder if they even knew that Venice was having problems.

His thoughts of Venice continued. The city was full of history that most tourists did not even have time to see. Most came, saw, ate, and left, as was the norm. Venice used to be resplendent. There was room for politics, for opulence, for religion, and entertainment. Marco remembered that Venetians had open minds and the city had open doors once, but it seemed impossible to think about that now. The city had such an open mind—they had a red light district, found right in the middle of San Polo around the Ponte delle Tette, which crossed the small canal running between Campo San Polo and the small Campo San Cassiano. This was a red-light district of sorts, a place where ladies of the night used to attract and lure in customers. Now it was just a little bridge, like so many others in the city. Nobody knew about it. It seemed that the world had become more puritan, and tried to hide the red light district as well as sexual conversation in general, but those things were very human in their essence.

That bridge was not the only one related to an area in Venice, one that showed what was going on in that district. The Ponte dei Pugni crossing

Rio San Barnaba in Dorsoduro, where people fought for entertainment and money, was another. What about the Ponte Chiodo in Cannaregio, where people were overturned into the water? Or the Ponte dei Sospiri, the "bride of sighs," which famously linked the doges' Palace to its interrogation rooms. Prisoners crossing that bridge would sigh as they looked through its window because they knew that it may be the last time they were ever going to see the sun again. Those who entered that prison never left; the cells on the lower levels would flood every time there was high tide, and the prisoners would drown in their cells. Marco could not imagine what that would be like. The prisoners sighing at that window must have felt that they were taking their last breath. Maybe death and love has something in common—they both take your last breath away. Quite suddenly, his thoughts drifted to his mystery woman, Beatrice. *Where was she in all of this history?*

CHAPTER 28

SOCIETY AND ITS MORALITIES

Marco was late for his meeting at Cricket's house. And that wasn't the worst of it. On his way, he stepped in a large pile of dog crap, which made him even later. He was mad not only about what happened to him but the fact that the owner of that dog should have been cleaning up after his pet. That was what most decent people would do. Was Venice at last filled to the brim with indecent folks?

"What are we discussing today?" Marco asked as he walked through the front door, left open. The students all turned to look at him.

"What's it mean to be a good citizen?" one of them said, raising an eyebrow at Marco.

"You may have to sit this one out, Marco," said Cricket, entering the room with his ever-present coffee mug in hand. "You see, friends, Marco here is constantly thinking about what it means to be a good citizen, and so the sides are not balanced."

"I'll take the opposite side of the debate if that helps."

"Your prerogative," said Cricket, adding with a wink, "although I'm not sure you're capable of stepping outside of your heart for a moment."

Marco smiled and sat down cross-legged among the students. "What makes for a good citizen? Easy. A reason for being." He then crossed his arms and looked into his lap. "I doubt many Venetians are aware of their reason for being here."

Again, the debate surged and tossed like an unmoored ship. A thin student from the University of Padova named Gregorio advocated for a more rigorous literary education to foster empathy.

Giuseppe, a modern day hippie, with his dour face under long, wild, curly hair, his thick glasses, and a sweatshirt that didn't match his pants, sat with a reluctance to speak.

Daniela, a small blond girl with small glasses that just surrounded her deep brown eyes, and thousands of freckles covering her face, sided with Marco and echoed most of his arguments.

Joseph, who had yet to speak, surprised the others when he blurted out, "What about Stoicism?"

"We all live in one country," said Gregorio, his brow furrowed, his voice earnest. "Our country gives us our home, our community, even our identity. It gives us everything. We are bound by duty to be a good citizen. There are some responsibilities of a good citizen that every person must follow. These responsibilities don't only improve our surroundings but also give us an inner sense of participating in something bigger than ourselves. A good citizen is one who is helpful and open-minded. He stays calm and doesn't make the lives of others harder. He helps others in every way possible. He is fair and just towards his neighbors. He must—"

Daniele interrupted him. "A good citizen is not a mischief maker." Her eyes glanced over at Marco, then back at the others. "The thing that makes any person a good citizen is helping others. He doesn't make waste and he abides by all the rules and laws of the country." Daniela's fiery energy soon fizzled out as she came to a realization, and then she said quietly, "But how to make this happen..."

The students were silent as they pondered the answer.

"Well, if you ask me," Cricket said, as he entered the conversation for the first time, "I'd say the solution is to live in accord with nature, which may be translated in the human sense as to live according to *reason*."

Marco sighed heavily. "If that could be achieved, then saving Venice would be easy."

——

It was late, and Marco had to go back to Venice. He shook hands with all and left. He went home with a goal—he would write letters to all the critical and influential people, even if he did not know them. He needed something to happen—a gesture of love, a plan of action. He and Venice needed something to show the wizard that Venetians were worthy of his trust. He needed to look behind human incongruity to find a chink in this wall of indifference.

——

Once home, Marco ate quickly.

"Marco, how do you feel?" his mother asked him. "You seem sad and worried. Is it something at school?"

Marco told his mother the story of the wizard, without mentioning the statue of Manin. He did not want her to worry that he was afraid of the statue that was right outside their front door. When he was through, she smiled and gave him a long hug without saying anymore.

"Do you really think someone is out to destroy Venice, as you said?" she said with level tone.

"Absolutely. Do you notice the graffiti, the popups on the floor, the urine in the corners, the fact that most of our business are owned by strangers? I bet someone will come and punish us, the Venetian, because we messed up, because we were not able to take care of ourselves and our city." He added without irony, "And may God help us when that finally happens."

CHAPTER 29

HOW TO SAVE VENICE

Time had been passing, and nothing had happened as a result of all of Marco's meetings with the mayor. Nor had any of his private conversations with friends and colleagues gotten him anywhere. Despondent and frustrated, he was determined to write a letter, but to whom?

Perhaps he could write to different people or groups or organizations. His first challenge in writing the letter was to decide what was important. Nobody would believe the story about the wizard, he was certain of that. Finally, he reduced his thoughts to where each person lived, envisioning the troubles in their areas. So, one letter might go to the mayor and his administrators, where he would ask each person involved to do *something* to make their alley better. His second letter would go the merchant association where he could ask shop owners to keep their walls clean and in good repair. He would send the third letter to animal control asking them to keep the cat population in check, ditto for the pigeons and rats polluting St. Mark Square. A fourth letter would go to the environmental section demanding a thorough cleaning of the canal on a regular basis, and to devise a plan for keeping that way.

Marco got to work on his letters. He asked the environmental services to take better care of the monuments like the Basilica of St. Mark and the Mori, the large clock in the square with two statues that hit a large bell at the hours and had been doing so for centuries. He asked the art section to restructure and preserve all the arts in Venice.

After writing the letters, he had another idea. He thought that Venice might need to have a City Manager, like so many cities in the United States. He gave up on that idea, knowing that the Italian bureaucracy was based on the old proverb, "He who goes slowly, goes safely and goes far." It was precisely this lassitude that spelled the end of Venice. Maybe he himself should be the City Manager. He knew the town, he knew the problems, he knew whose ears were most open. To handle the finances, well, he could always hire a financial officer for that. Yes, he would be the first City Manager of Venice, he decided. He had ambition and drive enough for the job. But would they take him seriously? He was only twenty.

Meeting Giorgio later, they went for Ombra and a Cicchetto. Marco knew his friend enjoyed his musings on Venice, despite jokes alluding to the contrary. But Marco also knew that there was some truth to Girogio's jabs. His words made Giorgio uncomfortable. Tonight was going to be one of those nights.

"So," said his friend, "a wizard, did you say? It's not enough that you need to save Venice by your own devices, now you need a wizard to get it done? Have you lost all hope? If you don't tone it down, they'll open up the old psychiatric hospital in San Servolo just for you."

At this, Marco looked at his friend in shock. Giorgio did not take him seriously at all. He decided that, at least for now, he would focus on the issues at hand and leave the wizard out of it. But now, he knew was truly alone, and his despair threatened to overtake him. He need to focus. They were sitting outside their favorite Bacaro just under the Rialto Bridge.

"Giorgio, how about this? Would you mind listening to my speech? I wrote it, but I need practice. I am getting ready to speak in front of people, important people, that might help Venice. I want to be sure they know what is going on. I also need to incorporate not only facts, but history and other things."

Looking away, Giorgio nodded his head. "Prattle on, dear brother."

Marco forged ahead despite this. He looked down at his written speech. He cleared his throat.

"My fellow Venetians, I am here to speak with you today about the problems of our dear city. Venice is sinking. She has slipped five inches in the last century. At the same time, the Adriatic has risen as much as four inches. These numbers may sound small, but the consequences are not. More than a hundred times a year now, the campi and campielli are flooded by high tides. The project MOSE should have been the solution but did not fix anything. Now, the name comes from Moses, of course, whom God sent to help the Jews escape to the Promised Land. We all know how Moses held back the waters of the Red Sea. Moses could certainly secure Venice from the high tide, but it's debatable whether God will send him back to help us." He noticed his friend nodding. "Giorgio, are you with me?" He was annoyed that is friend appeared to be lost in some other thought or fancy.

"I'm listening, I'm listening, go ahead," said Giorgio, yawning and rudely stretching out as if to take a nap, his long legs in the aisle.

Marco continued anyway. "It seems that everybody is waiting for Venice to die. This is the time of cholera, of that great secular prophet Thomas Mann, of the foul sickness and demise of von Aschenbach in 'Death in Venice.'" He nudged Giorgio with his foot, trying to keep him awake. "Now, the deadly bacteria are the tourists. The rapacious tourist culture is threatening Venice's existence, making Venice the new Disneyworld where people come like packs of wolves to feed and leave behind their excrement. Oh, their money is worth something to us, alright. It's worth trash, empty bottles, and cans on the ground and other problems to resolve. They show no respect for an old lady like Venice. Perhaps they are not much different from a lot of Venetians." Marco threw this line directly at his friend, who was tucked down into his seat, allowing the insult to fly over his head.

Marco continued. "Tourism has been tearing apart Venice's social fabric, cohesion, and civic culture for years. There were more than 2,400 hotels and bed and breakfasts, but they no longer satisfy the travel industry's appetites. The total number of guest quarters in Venice's historic center could reach 50,000 and take it over entirely."

Giorgio blinked his eyes slowly, almost in a dream state, but Marco continued.

"Just along the Grand Canal, Venice's main waterway, there have been many closures of state institutions, judicial offices, banks, the German Consulate, medical practices, and stores to make way for more hotels. What you think of my letter, up to this point?" asked Marco.

Giorgio did not answer.

Marco kicked his foot. "Hey."

"What is it?"

"What do you think so far?"

"You're a poet, what can I say?"

Marco sneered at him. "You're in your own little world right now."

"I swear, I'm listening. It flows well. You are getting the point across."

Ignoring the tone of his friend's voice, Marco continued.

"Local people have been pushed from the town. There are no jobs except in hotels, and local businesses are disappearing expect the ones connected with tourism. Venice is becoming a place where only old couples stay to die in their town. Young people are going out to the lands around Venice's outskirts to find a house and a job. The housing issue is becoming worse. To fix an apartment in Venice is so expensive that even the people who own houses refuse to update and keep it nice. They find it much cheaper to live outside Venice. Only the wealthy buy homes in Venice. And if you look at the phone book listings, a third of them are comprised of international names..."

As Marco finished, he looked up from his paper to see that Giorgio had fallen fully asleep in his chair. He folded up his letter and gave his friend a farewell wave, knowing it wouldn't be noticed. There he left his snoring friend, resolving to make a difference, with or without support. He was truly alone now, his only friends the ghosts of his beloved city.

CHAPTER 30

RAISING AWARENESS

The next morning, Marco met Mayor Ongaro at their regular café meeting spot in Campo San Luca. People from all walks of life assembled at that little place which made the place into a kettle of confined, excited atoms, and therefore a great spot to measure the pulse of the city.

"I have been thinking about a solution," Marco said. He looked up to see the mayor was smiling broadly. "What is it?"

"Have you noticed I've not said a single word to you since we sat down ten minutes ago? A full ten minutes you were outwardly silent. There must be a cacophony on the inside."

Marco smiled sheepishly. "You're right, sir. But all I have come up with so far is writing letters to each sector of the municipality. Writing to the town's benefactors is the next step."

"And what will that accomplish?"

Marco could tell Ongaro was feeling feisty.

"Funding to save our arts and buildings."

"Okay, go on."

"Well, finally, I'll write to the politicians in Rome and ask for support in planning."

The mayor out a hand to his chin. He had a full beard and mustache, and small, modern-looking glasses. He had a big nose that sloped, which caused glasses to slide down and balance at the end of it. His ears had hair coming out in tufts from its orifices, and his hair was not well groomed as should have suited a mayor. He looked more like a philosophy professor, more at home with gentlemen like old Cricket than suit-stuffed sycophants in a politician's office.

Ongaro set his Cornetto down. "It is a noble start, but you will receive a lot of silence by way of response. The few actual responses you get will either be empty promises or entreaties to stop 'being foolish' or to 'grow up and to accept reality.' I have fought many political battles in my time, being quite vocal about it. But it has cost me. My party in Rome does not like me because they know what I am going to say. They know what I demand, and they know that they cannot deliver it. Politicians are not in office to get results. They are in office to have and to maintain power, and that requires compromise. Unfortunately, it is our lives that get compromised. You and I don't care which party gets credit for keeping Venice safe from the high tide, but they care so much that they will stop all efforts until that credit goes where the majority wants it to go."

"Then what do I do?" shouted Marco, suddenly realizing that his voice had carried over the din of the place. He tucked his chin and frowned. "I am at a loss." Ongaro put a hand on his shoulder. "Go out into the streets. Talk to the *people*. Get them worked up and angry. I'm sure you will find that most Venetians still love Venice. With enough voices shouting, Rome must listen. While you do that, I will get you an invitation to go to Rome and observe the parliament to see what they do. Okay? This coming week they will be talking about funding for Venice. What do you say? That will be the perfect time for you to sit on the viewer's bench and learn how they operate."

"That is outstanding!" Marco said, feeling a sense of mania mixing uncomfortably with his depression.

The mayor held up one finger. "Now, just a moment, before you go and entertain delusions of grandeur, you must remember: If you think you will change the world in that one day, you are wrong. You will leave feeling frustrated and angry and hopeless. I am telling you this not as some oracle set before you to turn your fate. I am preparing you as I would a friend who is about to embark on a perilous journey. Understand? So, go anyway. Learn the contours of the battlefield. I will set it up for you." The mayor waved his hand wearily, took a sip of his coffee, and Marco noticed his hand shake a little as he held the cup.

Marco didn't want to say anything, but he wondered if his mentor's health was not at its peak. Then he shook his head in determination and looked the mayor directly in the eye. "I will go. Maybe I will come home defeated, but I am going to give it everything I have."

"Not maybe. You *will* be defeated, but only in the purpose you thought you had a moment ago. You will not be defeated in this other, more ephemeral purpose."

Marco thought he picked up a sigh emitting from the man's lips, but maybe it was his imagination. He hoped the mayor shared his enthusiasm and excitement, but he suspected otherwise.

———

That very afternoon, Marco enlisted the secretary to the Dean at the University of Venice to help him create a flier to distribute around Venice. In it, he documented the deterioration of the city and asked the citizens to own up to their duty to take care of their home. And it detailed what efforts were required to fix the city.

The next day, walking in Calle Dei Fabbri, he strolled toward the Rialto Bridge, stopping in Campo San Bartolomeo. As he distributed the fliers, he saw that some people read them with interest while others dropped them on the ground and walked away. The irony was not lost on Marco.

After distributing fliers through Campo St. Margherita, he took Rio Dei Greci and ended up in Riva Degli Schiavoni. The canal ended there, and the lagoon extended to the island of Lido. He kept distributing more fliers and getting more and more disappointed as people either waved him off or tossed the flyer on the ground after barely glancing at it. He planned to cover Venice on that first day and then the other islands on the next day, but the early efforts did not seem promising.

Was he contributing to the litter of the city? That was a question he was not prepared to begin contemplating. Perhaps this was an exercise in counterirritation. He had to leave it at that to preserve his sanity.

By suppertime, the only things motivating Marco were his dreams of traveling to Rome and visiting the parliament. He told his parents about the plan to go and they happily supported him. He went from dinner directly to bed. After hours of tossing and turning, he decided to get up and take a walk. He took some comfort in the lateness of the hour.

He walked to the Academia passing the wooden bridge, seeing his flyers scattered everywhere. He picked them up when he could.

He stopped to look at the church dedicated to the Virgin Mary, who'd saved Venice from the plague.

Even the most powerful memories of the community never seemed to last more than a couple of generations. The people of Venice had all but forgotten the plagues of 1577 and 1630. Even the most severe disasters could be relegated to impersonal history. Even the festival in honor of the Virgin every November 21st didn't jar people's memories. To them, it was just another day to drink and eat and pollute.

When was the next plague to come. And who would come bearing it?

Once again, his mind did not allow him the luxury of contemplation on this question.

Shadows hid the city's secrets, and so Marco avoided them as best he could. Exhausted, he finally found himself standing at the foot of the statue of Manin.

"I don't know what to do, Signore. I am failing Venice. I am failing you! People don't understand what is important anymore." After a moment of grief-laden reflection, he asked, "What is going to wake them up?"

CHAPTER 31

THE WINGED LION BACK IN TIME

Manin knew he had to do something to help his young friend. The winged lion that lay at his feet moved its massive head to look at Marco. Its eyes shone with intelligence and glowed as brightly as Manin's face glowed. It stood and slowly walked over to him. Marco tentatively reached up to stroke the big cat's mane. Unlike the statue of Manin, it had the look and feel of a real lion, only with wings. The beast gently buzzed each of Marco's cheeks in the classic Italian greeting, then it lay down low in front of Marco expectantly, looking back at him. Marco understood and mounted the beast. The lion stood up and beat its wings.

As they took to the air, the ground below them dissolved and re-formed before Marco's eyes. He watched the Festa Della Sensa where he saw people dancing and drinking in the squares. As they flew on, he saw the doge Pietro II Orseolo freeing the denizens of Dalmatia from the Slavs. He was traveling through time. This was the year 999. Then he saw doge Ziani signing the Treaty of Venice in the presence of the Pope and the Holy Roman Emperor, Frederick Barbarossa. They had slipped into 1177.

They flew in large, gentle circles around Venice, watching scene after scene changing. He saw parties flourishing in every campo and campiello; he saw ceremonies, shows, harlequins, and storytellers in St. Mark's Square; he saw markets with goods of all kinds from every country on earth. He watched as wooden buildings were erected for special occasions, and vast crowds of Venetians and non-Venetians alike milled about between stalls and cafes. This was the most famous of Venice's festivals, the one that people the world over associate with the great city. This was Carnival, with the many parades of costumes in Piazza San Marco and its bell tower. The 'Festa Delle Marie,' with the beautiful young Venetian women selected by a jury and its parades of decorated floats, proceeded to the mainland. On the stage of honor, he saw doge Domenico Morosini, not Marino. It had to be the year 1150. He had led a winning battle against the Normans, and proclaimed that it was much like the fight with Attila.

As they flew to the next scene, Marco became dizzy with the speed with which time passed beneath them. Now he was looking down upon doge Contarini, one of the fairest leaders Venice had ever known. The doge was waiting for boats to pass in front of him on the Grand Canal. Marco figured it had to be about the year 1601. The *Regatta Storica* had been a key event in the annual racing calendar of Venetian rowing, a sport practiced uniquely in the Venetian lagoon for over a thousand years. The long procession of dozens of genuine sixteenth-century boats with costumed figures and the doge leading it all with his wife and family was a spectacular sight for Marco to behold. The renderings in history books had not done it justice.

They flew over the island opposite to Saint Mark's square. There were no bridges there, but a person could walk from boat to boat to get cross. The canal was crowded with them. Thousands of boats functioned as bridges over the basin of San Marco. It was the feast of the Redentore on the night between the third Saturday and Sunday of July, celebrating the end of the 1577 plague. He watched the construction of the Basilica del Santissimo Redentore by Palladio on the island of the Giudecca. It rose like a house of cards collapsing in reverse.

The lion wavered a bit, as if to tip his wing, so that Marco could get a better look. He could feel the muscles of the beast beneath him. He could see the feast below, with an abundance of food—early traditional Venetian dishes. The aromas wafted up to him. Then the fireworks began exploding around them, great flashes and reports that obliterated his senses in a volley of exquisite assaults. In the large boat, he could see another doge, Francesco Dona, elected as an old, very wise man. Marco felt the man's benevolence just as certain as he had smelled the ancient food. He felt the man's tolerance for all religions, his love of the Jews, and that great people's advance in their social standing during his time.

The lion flew back to Piazza San Marco and landed at the foot of the statue. Marco dismounted, tears in his eyes. The lion gave him the same formal kisses from their greeting, returned to its place next to Manin, and was once again bronze.

Once home, Marco didn't fall asleep for hours. His heart pounded hard in his chest as he absorbed all that he had seen. When sleep finally did come, it was without dreams. No dream, after all, could compete.

CHAPTER 32

THE VENETIAN ISLANDS

He awoke with a strong urge to see open space.

After breakfast, he took the vaporetto to visit all of Venice. The water bus took him out into the open lagoon. In Murano, he saw dozens of tourists visiting the glass factories.

In a rare fit of compassion, he approached them. "Where are you visiting from?"

"We are from Milan," said a woman clinging to what Marco assumed was her husband. It's our first time in Venice. Yes, we are here to see the laces."

Marco corrected them. "You mean the glasses. You are in Murano not in Burano"

"What's the difference?" said the husband, whose eyes were hidden by mirrored sunglasses. "Six of one, half a dozen of the other, right?"

Marco smiled, though his face felt tight. "Actually, the islands each have their difference and soul, and we need to keep their souls in order to keep Venice alive."

"You are a freaky young man," the woman said, ending the sentence in a drunken chuckle.

So much for his compassion.

He came to realize that his compassion was for the ideal of humanity. It was for what the human race was *capable* of becoming. Not for what it was.

He continued to try to talk to other people about taking care of Venice, but his talk always fell on deaf ears.

He came across a man helping at the embarcadero, speaking only the local dialect.

"Hello, what about singing a lyric about saving Venice today?"

The guy stared at Marco. "*Ma va nella mona va,*" was his rude reply.

Other workers Marco reached out to returned equally dismal results. None could hear that Venice needed care. Torcello and Burano were much the same.

He had one bit of respite in Burano, however, when an elderly man beckoned him over.

"Young man, come over here and tell me about the state of Venice."

Marco wondered whether the old man was calling him over to mock him, as it seemed like that could be a lively pastime for an old Venetian. There was only one way to tell.

He went over to the old man: "Good afternoon, Signor. It would be my honor to talk with you. Thank you."

The gentleman had to be at least 80, but he was sharp-minded and in good health. Marco would not be surprised to learn that he still rowed his boat on the canal every morning. He was sitting at an outside table of a local restaurant enjoying the warm afternoon sun and sipping his ombra.

When Marco sat, the old man ordered the same for him and said, "You say that Venice is dying? Could it be true that I am no longer the only person in Venice to see this? I have seen both world wars. I have seen much in this life. Venice has not changed, not at her heart, but the people..." he paused, choked up with emotion. "The people have changed, and it is very much for the worse. People have always been greedy and fearful, even apathetic, but now they express these terrible sides of themselves with pride. They are proud to be ignorant. It is almost as though they were under the spell of a curse. I fought to make the world a better place. Look at Burano. The young leave and only the old remain until God calls us home."

A single tear glistened in the old man's eyes. Marco was rapt with attention.

A spark of hope renewed in his heart.

"Tell me your story, young man," the old man said. "We all know Venice is dying. That is not to be disputed. I would like to know *why* you think Venice will die?"

CHAPTER 33

THE OLD MAN AND FORGOTTEN LULLABIES

For the first time, Marco decided not to hold back and instead let his heart pour out. He told the old man about his experience with the living statue of Daniele Manin, about the Wizard of Tribuka, and about Merlin and Morgan le Fay. He told him of the curse and the pact. He even told the gentleman of his ride on the lion's back, journeying through the history of Venice.

"Memories!" the old man declared when Marco was done. A tear ran down his cheek. "You have awakened memories from my youngest days. My grandfather told me these same stories. He died when I was just about the age you are now. Then the war came. I got lost in the never-ending battles, the loss of so many lives, the dramatic changes in life that came after World War Two had ended, and I forgot all about those stories. I never told them to my children." He pulled out a battered handkerchief dabbed at his face. "My entire generation forgot to keep the sacred stories of Venice."

Marco let the old gentleman finish in his own time. Then they finished their wine in silence.

"I hope we can avert the end of *this* story," said Marco. "I still believe that man is good. I have to believe that."

"You believe or you hope?" the old man said, then waved away the answer before it came. "Never mind. You are young yet and your optimism is needed if Venice is to be saved. As for me," He pounded his chest. "I no longer believe in man. Man will do whatever feels good unless someone guides him to do right." He then gave Marco a long appraising look and said, "You are a good man.

"After the major war and a minor one involving my heart, I grew bitter, I treated everyone with indifference, thinking only about myself. I drank heavily. And you know what? I got a job on the team that restored Piazza San Marco."

"No kidding!"

"Indeed. And over time, the work healed my soul, and I stopped getting drunk every night. I saw so many tourists every day. I started noticing how much people like Venice and how lucky we were to live in this paradise. Tourists would stop us and ask about our work, and about the city. We became informal tour guides. Even today most Venetians act as tour guides for the tourists."

Marco nodded knowingly as the old man's eyes began to light up again slowly.

"One day there was a group of tourists asking us questions," he said. "It was a very hot day. Nobody who was not accustomed to it should have been out in that heat. A very pretty girl about my age fainted, and I bent to help her. I gave her water. Six months later, we married. She loved me for *me*. She gave me two beautiful children and a happy life. My parents wanted me to marry a Venetian girl. She was from Padova. But they learned to love her, too. She has been my companion and my best friend for over sixty years now. God sent her to save my soul." He paused, and sighed, a pleasant exhaling of soft breath mingling with the Venetian air.

"I'm sorry," he said with a humble grin. "I ramble on. Do not lose hope, young man. Remember the apostles didn't have the friendliest audiences, either."

The old man stood and looked past Marco to the sidewalk beyond. He smiled a happy smile. "There she is, my gift from God, my Beatrice."

Marco's heart stopped. An elegant old woman with hair like snow walked slowly toward them with a wooden cane. She was wonderful to look at, as if her beauty came with effort. She gave Marco a polite smile as she approached her husband for a kiss. The old man introduced them, and Marco kissed her hand. He then hugged the old man, thanking him for the gift of restored faith.

As Marco returned home, he couldn't help but shiver a bit with happiness. This was the first time someone had believed him, accepted his message, and even confirmed the legend. What Manin had told him of the Wizard of Tribuka was true. Fathers had been passing it down to sons for ages. War had stopped the flow of the legend in the old man's family. Marco wondered if that was the case for all of Venice. He wondered why his father didn't know of the legend.

He resolved to give his story to the world.

PART III

———•———

CHAPTER 34

GOING TO ROME

He was eager to tell the mayor about his visit with the old man in Burano the previous day, so he went to the cafe where his friend and mentor spent much of his days. The mayor had been reading the newspaper. He showed it to Marco. Marco's letter had been published. A sidebar had an article about his flier distribution. It was making fun of him and of his desire to save Venice, with mention that in an effort to end Venice's litter, he'd contributed to it.

"Try not to let it get under your skin," the mayor told him. "You're doing the right thing. Also, there is good news. I received the approval for you to visit parliament while they are discussing funding for Venice. You will need to take the night train tonight to get there early. You will need to go to Montecitorio, the seat of the Italian Chamber of Deputies. You will need to go there to get accredited and be ready for the next day. Come to my office. My secretary will have a letter for you to present at Montecitorio."

"I don't know what to say."

Ongaro smiled. "You can say nothing for a change. Oh, remember, get to Montecitorio before noon. For in the afternoon, nothing happens. You're lucky if you find someone who wants to do anything."

"What do you mean."

Ongaro gave his characteristic dismissive wave. "State jobs are difficult to lose. It's virtually impossible to fire you, so there is not much motivation to work. This is another disease of our society, Marco. Everybody takes advantage of the government, not realizing they are exploiting themselves and their neighbors. But I go on. Good luck, and let me know what you felt about the debate."

Marco thanked the mayor and told him of his visit with the old man in Burano, speaking only of the legends and leaving out his own personal association with them. He didn't want the mayor to think he had lost his mind and started talking to statues. The Mayor said he did not know of such a legend, but perhaps Marco should write another letter to the newspaper asking the old men of Venice if any of them remembered the story. Marco liked that idea. He would do that. After they left the cafe, he went to his college to study for an exam he had coming up.

———

After lunch, Marco went to the train station and purchased a ticket for that night's train with a sleeping berth. Then he went to Ca' Farsetti, where the mayor's office was. The mayor's secretary smiled when she saw Marco, and confided in him that she the promise of a bright future in him.

"So, you're off to Rome?" she teased. "I've always wanted to see Rome. Everywhere you turn you can see history. The trip will be something to remember, Marco."

"I'll tell you all about it."

"I'll hold you to it," she said, and handed him the letter.

———

From the Stazione Termini in Rome, he walked a few blocks to get a room. He kept his eyes open and hungry. Rome was filled with signs of decay and corruption everywhere. Around him, people slept in the train station, begged for money, and there were prostitutes on street corners. People were exchanging little plastic baggies with white powder and pills for money in front of the bordello. He had heard this was common in big cities, but he never really believed it until he saw it in person.

So, it wasn't only Venice. The plague had hit other parts of Italy as well.

He found a bed and breakfast to stay in. The room was clean, and it had a sink. The bathroom was outside and served five other rooms. He put his stuff down, took a shower, and got ready to get his pass for the day after.

CHAPTER 35

A PASS TO THE CHAMBER OF THE DEPUTY

He arrived at 8:30 a.m. sharp. But it was almost noon before he was received.

"Let's do this quickly," said the official, a twittery fellow who stank of cologne and cigarettes. "In ten minutes I'm going to eat. You're lucky that you can travel from Venice. Otherwise, I might not have seen you until after lunch." The man giggled at his joke.

Marco was puzzled. He had been sitting outside the office since 9 a.m. and he didn't see anybody going in or out. What was this official possibly doing all day? The man made a pass in the form of a little tag and gave him a form letter for his entrance at Montecitorio the next day. Marco thanked the man and left feeling as though he'd just been processed into a system.

Having been sitting for what felt like forever, Marco needed to walk. He'd never seen Rome before. He decided to give himself a tour.

He found himself not far from the Trevi Fountain when he turned toward the Pantheon. There he found a takeaway pizza place. He ordered pizza with potatoes, knowing it was a specialty in Rome, and a Coke. He sat on the steps of the Pantheon to eat. The Pantheon was the best-preserved building from the ancient days of Rome. He reminded himself how the Pantheon had been completed around the year 125 in the reign of Hadrian and was created for the emperor to address his subjects from a place equaling that of the Gods.

He had just put himself in A.D. 125, the era of Hadrian's reign, to witness the dedication of the Pantheon when he spied an attractive girl sitting on the steps just a few feet from him. She was eating a slice of pizza, too. Every time she took a bite, she emanated joy, chewing slowly with her eyes closed, as if the experience reminded her of a lover. With short brown hair and marble-like skin, she was the most beautiful girl that Marco had ever seen. She had a book poised face-down on her lap.

He nearly swooned when he saw the title.

La Vita Nova.

Marco's heart went to his throat.

He got up and walked around her like a tourist appraising the very essence of the place.

There was the scent of Fendi coming off her.

He was unable to speak.

CHAPTER 36

LA VITA NOVA

The girl looked at him and smiled. "If I have a hair out of place, you'd better not mention it. I have delicate sensibilities."

"I'm sorry," said Marco, entranced at the green of her eyes. "I don't mean to stare. I was impressed by your choice of reading material. Also, I hope I'm not being forward, but I was taken by what appears to be your joy of life. Even in a city such as this."

"Well, you know the American saying, don't you? When in Rome...?"

"How does it end?" he said. "Do as the pigeons do?"

She laughed. "I believe that's it. Which is why I'm sitting here with enjoying a scrap of food. You from Rome?"

"Venice. We have tons of pigeons."

"Venice! I love it. You're lucky to live there. I absolutely adore Venice. I was there a few months ago, but only for a short weekend with my family. I wish I could have stayed longer and admired all the beauty."

"It has beauty for sure. One day it will be underwater."

"Mmm," she said, pursing her lips and staring into the distance. I suppose it is a pity you can't fix the problems of the high tide. I come from a line of art lovers, you know."

For a moment, Marco became somber.

"I'm sorry, did I say something rude?" she said.

"No," he replied. "You're right. I'm very lucky to have grown up in Venice. It's just that I'm here to see parliament tomorrow as they decide what money to spend to help Venice clean itself up—the hide tide problem included."

"I've known about the problem with the high tide," she said. "I remember reading that at times it can have high as a meter and more, sometimes up to five feet. Probably a good time to invest in the goloshes industry."

Despite his anxieties, Marco couldn't help but find the dark joke musing. "I think you may be more forward-thinking than most Venetians. But you're right. And your investment would peak in November and December, when the tides are at their highest. As of now, the high waters usually affect only the lowest parts of the town, such as St. Mark's Square."

"Interesting," she said, putting a hand onto the back of her neck as she tilted her head toward him. "How do Venetians deal with it?"

"We're used to coping with *acqua alta*. We get these alerts by text messages. At the same time, elevated platforms are set along the main streets to allow passage. Public waterbuses keep on working, although some lines may be subject to changes. In any case, access to most of the town is guaranteed. And you're right about galoshes. *Acqua alta* boots are a must. But you want to know the funny part? The time it takes to set up these inconveniences is about as long as it takes for the water to recede, making the whole endeavor a farce."

She shook her head. "I can't imagine what that must be like."

"Well, *acqua Alta* can be dealt with. It's an inconvenience at worst, a charming quirk of the city at best. All you have to do is wait a few hours for the tide to ebb. I'm more worried about the altimetric loss and the effects of climate change. I'm not confident we can fix those. I could give you all the wonderful scientific stuff that makes me sound smart, but really, in short, Venice is sinking."

"That really is tragic," she said with a sympathetic lilt to her voice. "I mean, that's your home. I'm sorry for being callous and making jokes."

Marco smiled. "No, I think it helps. People tell me I'm too serious. Humor is a way of navigating the rough areas of life." He paused to reflect on what he'd just said. "I guess I need to remember that."

"Also, remember the reason why bread never has problems."

"Why is that?"

"Because it rises."

Marco threw his head back in a laugh. He then held up his pizza. "Salut."

"Salut," she said, and tapped his half-finished slice with hers.

They chatted about small things between bites. And when they were finished, Marco slapped at his head. "Here I am prattling on and on and I haven't even asked you your name."

"You haven't told me yours. We're even."

He held out his hand. "I'm Marco."

She wiped her hand on her lap and clasped his. "Genevieve."

"Pleased to meet you. If you don't mind me saying, you don't seem to be from here."

She winked at him. "Was it something I said?"

He held up a hand. "Please don't take that as an insult. You speak perfect Italian. I could just tell. You have an air about you."

"Belgium. Specifically, Antwerp."

"I love the Belgian people."

"Then, Marco, my friend, I am afraid you are out of luck. My Father is Dutch and my mother is French."

"Ha! That's where you're wrong. I love the Dutch and the French too. What brings you to Rome?"

She pointed to the book, which now lay by her side. "Good reading light here."

He laughed. It felt so good. "For real."

"Okay, for real. I came to Rome for my semester of studying abroad. Also, to perfect my Italian. You can't order a good slice of pizza without that. Anyway, I love Italy. Art, sun, water, wonderful food. It's an amazing place."

"It's only the birthplace of the Renaissance. Nothing special," he said, realizing her humor was catching. "What are you studying?"

"Architecture," she said.

"You've come to the right place."

"Rome is fascinating. But I must confess, I wanted to see Venice."

"You're joking."

"Totally serious," she said. "From what you've been telling me, it seems I'd best hurry. While we're on the subject of you talking, you speak like a man of letters. What do you do?"

"Just an eternal student. Like Trofimov in *The Cherry Orchard*. I'm studying Philosophy and Journalism in school. I would love to show you

Venice some time. This is the first time I've been to Rome, though, so I can't give you a tour here, I'm afraid."

"Oh, and here I was all set to pay you the standard rate. How about this? Why don't I give *you* a tour of Rome and then we'll talk about that Venice tour?"

"It's a deal," he said. "Now, about Dante."

She picked up the book. "I'm not sure why it attracts me so. I mean, it was an innovative poem for its time. But really, I think I like it because it's a true love story. Is that banal?"

"Not at all. May I see your book?"

She handed it to him and he opened it.

He had expected to see what he saw there now, and was not the least bit startled by it. He smiled at the same handwritten notes, the same handwriting, and the waft of her that came off its pages. It was returning home after a long voyage. Or to childhood and to dreams. Nothing unexpected, but everything magical and perfectly in his place.

"What are you smiling at?" she said.

"I think Dante is playing a game with me."

She screwed up her face in amusement. "How so?"

"Well, I came here because my city is dying and nobody seems to care. And the minute I laid eyes on you, I decided in that moment that I'd had enough wallowing in my anxieties. And it was all because of this book." He tapped the cover.

"I'll remember to thank Dante when I see him in the afterlife," she said, rising. "Now, *Signore*, the tour begins!"

CHAPTER 37

TWIN FLAME SOUL

They started at the Piazza Navona, then they went to Piazza di Spagna, taking a jog up and down the Spanish steps. He found Genevieve easygoing, quick to rise to a dare, and always positive. They walked on to the Colosseum. Marco had always been fascinated by the history those ruins communicated to him, but in this moment, he could not immerse himself in thoughts about the Colosseum, because his heart and soul were completely taken by Genevieve.

He did wonder for a brief moment, however, whether his history obsessions were merely a diversion from his lonely life. But that was his former self thinking. He did indeed begin to imagine that he had two selves—the one before Genevieve and the one after, forged by her.

They held hands. They ran. They told each other funny stories from their lives. He felt so inexplicably comfortable with her. But it did not take long for her to appear as if she noticed there was a side of Marco that she could not access. He seemed to be carrying a burden alone. He hoped she wouldn't probe him on it. He couldn't befoul her with his concerns.

When they arrived at the Terme di Caracalla, she sat down to catch her breath and slapped her hands on her lap. "Okay, what's in a name?"

"Say that again?" he said, winded.

"*Marco*, names after the Venetian patron saint?"

He shrugged. "I guess is a popular name in Venice like Marco Polo. Do I look like him?" He turned to show her his profile.

"You need to work on your beard. Otherwise, a dead ringer."

"Your turn. Genevieve."

"Funny enough," she said, "my name belongs to a patroness of a city as well. My mother is from Paris and she loves history. As you know, in the past, women had no rights anywhere, including in France, so she was looking for a name that was a sign of strength. The name means 'God blessing' in French. She told me one day she was reading a history book when she found a section about the Saint Genevieve. She was the patroness of Paris who defended the city against Attila the Hun."

The name made him start for a moment.

"Are you okay?" she said, her face one of concern. "You look..."

"I'm fine," he said. "I'll tell you what Attila means to me some other time."

"Should I be scared that Attila brings such meaning to your life?"

"No," he said.

And then, as if he was destined to do so, he began to tell her, for the time to speak was the present. Love in his hands was a precious thing like china, and it was up to him to hold it so. He told Genevieve everything. About his campaign in Venice. About the Wizard and the imminent death of his city. He even told her about his experience with the statue of Manin and the lion. She paid close attention to him, responding appropriately, and encouraging him to continue.

When he finished, Genevive paused for a moment, biting her bottom lip.

"You probably think me a candidate for the nuthouse," he said.

"Not at all," she said. "It is an interesting story. Heartbreaking, even. And, God help me, the details are so vivid that I think your story is true." She smiled to drive honesty through her humor. "I don't care if it's impossible or not. I believe what you are saying. But tell me, how do we fight back against the Wizard of Tribuka?"

It had not been until this moment that he realized just how lonely this burden had been. Her hand appeared in his then, and he looked up into her eyes. He was fighting tears and his eyes were wet, but he didn't care. Then they were kissing.

When their lips parted. She said, "Kissing me? Is that how we save Venice?"

"No," he said, "but it will take an act of love just the same."

"Well, the first thing you need to do," she said, "is go to Parliament. Don't kiss anyone there."

"I won't," he said.

"Learn if they have any funding to allocate. And then you'll have to see if they have the capacity to love Venice like you do. And another thing. I want to help you. Do you accept?"

"Do I have a choice?"

"No, and neither do you have a choice whether or not to feed me."

They found a place to order a porchetta, another of the Roman specialties he so often heard about.

———

"I need to show you something," he said when his belly was full. "Would you come to my hotel?"

"Are you propositioning me, Saint Marco?"

He raised his right hand. "I swear it is completely innocent."

"Let me get my things."

They walked on into the night chatting, laughing, and reached her apartment. He waited for her in the lobby. She was quick, and when she came down, they pick up a taxi to get to Marco's hotel.

Marco got in his room and from his luggage took out the copy of the *La Vita Nova* he had picked up months ago. His heart bursting through his chest, he turned to her and said, "I think this is yours."

She took the book as if it were the product of a magic trick. "My God..."

"I have been looking and dreaming about you since I found it."

She gave him an incredulous look.

"I was hoping to find that you were a nice girl, but you are exceeding all my expectations. I think God wanted me to have the best present I have ever received in my life."

His soul spoke loudly in the small room.

They fell into bed and made love.

And they shared secrets, some spoken, some not.

CHAPTER 38

THE ITALIAN PARLIAMENT AND THE UNESCO REPORT

Marco had come to Rome to see if he could save Venice. But here he had found love. He felt a bit confused by everything that had happened so fast, but the confusion didn't last. He knew he had to let her go long enough to sit in parliament for the morning. He had never wanted to stay with someone so strongly in his life. As he put his suit on, she donned her jeans and a t-shirt. They walked together to Montecitorio.

Genevieve gave him a sweet kiss and a hug. "In Bocca al Lupo."

Marco smiled. "Crepi il lupo," he said. "So we are going to meet in front of St Peter's Church in the Vatican at lunchtime?"

She smiled reassuringly. "Of course, don't worry, I'll be there for you."

Now he knew it was true. She would be there. He watched her from behind as she walked off. Then she turned.

"Marco," she shouted, anxiously. "Can't I come in with you?"

He shrugged. "I'll ask!"

He found out from the clerk that yes, she could go in to the building with him, but she had to wait downstairs at the café since she did not have a pass. She assured Marco she was fine with that. After all, she had Dante to keep her company.

———

Marco showed his pass to the guard and entered the house of Parliament. He went to the frieze, located above the galleries for the authorities. He took in the building, which was like an amphitheater formed by benches sloping down towards the president's bench, the imposing arches of the galleries running around the entire hall, and the glass and iron velarium which illuminated the room.

Just as he took a seat on one of the benches, he saw the deputies enter the room. The president took a seat in the central part of the plenary hall, just below, by the two rows of government benches where the ministers sat.

On the same bench, to the right of the president, the deputy secretary sat down. To the left, the Secretary-General and officials in charge of the various technical activities that accompany parliament took their seats. The deputy took his place according to a longstanding tradition dating back to the French Revolution, the parliamentary groups sit in the House on the right, in the center or on the left according to which position they consider best reflects their political identity or historical tradition. They were ready to begin.

The funding and maintenance of Venice were not among the first few subjects of discussion.

But finally, the time came, and the leader of the opposition talked about the recent UNESCO report regarding the problems in Venice. The UNESCO meeting was just a month ago in Venice. Now, at the beginning of August, they had as yet received no feedback. The speaker began citing the research published by UNESCO during the meeting which was recently published, and which pointed an accusing finger at the lack of help the Italian government gave to Venice. It sounded like the people of UNESCO cared more about Venice than the people of Italy or even Venice itself.

It was during this time that Genevieve, with her French charm, must have been able to get a pass in order to enter the auditorium. Marco noticed her sitting in the back. She warmed his soul.

The ministers of arts, cultural heritage, and infrastructure began reading the UNESCO report to the assembly, detailing the findings and the lack of a viable solution.

"What about if we ask private people for funding and help," said a deputy from the right wing of the amphitheater.

The opposition leader shot him down with more facts and figures.

Marco felt a tug on his collar. When he turned, Genevieve was there right next to him. She left her hand for him on his lap and he took it. They looked in each other's eyes, and no words were necessary.

CHAPTER 39

RESTORING VENICE

"Then was anything done? *Is* anything being done?" asked a deputy from the minority group.

"I read the UNESCO report..." the president began. He then cleared his throat and outlined his interpretation.

During this long speech, Marco was suddenly conscious of Genevieve and how she must be taking all this mumbo jumbo. There's nothing like love to make one self-aware, he thought. He looked at her and noticed a confused expression on her face.

"You know Marco," she said, "if this were *my* country, we would already be acting on the issues. Do they want to help or not? And if they do, what can they do for real without hours of discussion?" She gave an ironic laugh. "I mean, really! This is like the world's longest nap."

"I know," Marco whispered, unable to help but smile at the absurdity of it. "This is my country, unfortunately, lots of talk, little fact." He smiled and shook his head.

"What is it?" she said.

"I think I finally found someone more upset about Venice than I am. I think I like you more and more by the minute."

"Has UNESCO addressed the problem of the high tide?" asked another deputy from the left wing.

"We should go and make love in bushes in the park," she whispered, causing him to blush.

"Stop that," he said, trying to control a boyish giggle from escaping his throat.

"What are the conclusions then? Is there any funding to help our government?"

"We could make love in the bushes and then go for gelato. We'll finish our gelato and hit the bushes again."

Marco let out a tiny laugh that made heads turn. He cleared his throat in an effort to disguise it. When he looked at Genevieve for reproach, her face was stern, as if she were one of his accusers. He put a finger to his lips and winked.

At that point, the opposition leader took the stand and said, "Dysfunction in the current government is to blame…"

"This, my dear colleagues," he concluded after several minutes, "is all the fault of our present government. It is truly incapable of preserving of our cultural heritage. We do not need UNESCO to tell us that the things do not work. We know it, and we need to act."

The assembly rumbled, and in the visitor's benches, everyone began talking at the same time.

"Silence, please," the assembly secretary called out, trying to bring calm in the assembly. But it was not working. The deputies were discussing and shouting at each other.

The majority leader said. "You are trying to hide your unsuitability, since you have been in power nothing happens, and our country is falling into ruin everywhere."

Marco turned to Genevieve. "See what we would have missed? No more of your foolish plans. This is getting exciting now!"

She gave his hand a squeeze and nuzzled in closer.

He felt like he could fly.

CHAPTER 40

POOR ATTITUDE

Arguing, accusations, and mayhem were coming in from all sides. Nothing was getting accomplished. Marco and Genevieve watched with astonishment.

"These are the people who lead your country?" she asked. "These are the ones that should make the country better? No wonder nothing ever happens or gets done. Instead of discussing business and solving problems, they go back to their quarrels, their interests, and their pride. A government should look after its people. But here they do not. They are actors in a grand theater of the absurd. And nobody goes off-script."

Marco could not answer her. He was ashamed of his own countrymen. Italy was such a wonderful country. Politics ruined everything.

It took quite a while for the assembly to calm down. When order was finally restored, the Minister of Cultural Heritage rose. "We need to vote on a resolution to set apart funding for Venice and start fixing according to the recommendations we have."

"Hear, hear," whispered Marco.

The place fell silent while they cast their votes.

The silence was interrupted by the secretary of the assembly: "I am sorry dear colleagues, but I was counting the deputies that are present right now, and we do not have enough to cast a vote. That was an oversight on my part."

The secretary asked the usher to see if some of them were outside drinking a coffee. The usher came back and said that there was no one outside. Ongaro was right. It was now close to lunchtime and nobody wanted to stay in assembly and perform a job for which they were elected and paid.

The secretary then said, "I'm sorry, but we need to put off the vote for another day, we need to find another day on the calendar."

Marco had had enough. He stood up. "It is not possible," he said, his voice booming. "How can this be possible?"

Everyone turned their heads to the visitor benches.

"How can you do this? I came from Venice in the hope that you would do something about our city and these are the results? Another delay, another day, week, month lost?"

Genevieve reached out and took Marco's hand to calm him down. He pulled it away.

"Do you realize" he said, "how many times you have postponed this vote? Do you realize that while you are talking Venice is dying in front of our eyes? Did any of you come to Venice to visit? Have any of you loved a place that is so unique as Venice? Venice is going to die, and you will be all responsible."

The deputies looked stunned.

"Go back to where you came from, little scoundrel," said a secretary, "before we have you arrested for inappropriate conduct and offense to public officials."

"Is that how you answer?" said Marco.

The secretary waved dismissively. "A little boy like you knows nothing of the world we live in. You know nothing about politics." He then narrowed his eyes, stood up, and pointed at Marco. "I bet your mommy raised you to expect everything to go your way. I bet you thought you could get everything you wanted. Just another entitled child."

Marco left the chamber in disgust.

A small group of journalists surrounded him then. They were interested in his story and asked a few questions. Flustered and still feeling the heat of rage and defeat, Marco answered as many as he could. He saw Genevieve step up next to him and was instantly ashamed of himself. He grabbed her hand and worked his way through the crowd. Once outside and down the stairs, they walked to Vatican City under a pall of dejection. Marco's head was spinning. Genevieve gave him a hug and a kiss, but she did not talk. They went together to St. Peter's Church.

They stopped in front of the Pieta.

"How ironic," he said. "Italians can generate such a masterpiece and then refuse to take care of the beauty of their own country. Venice will suffer like Christ. Only there is no resurrection for Venice." He turned to Genevieve. "I guess you realize now that I'm no saint."

"You're in luck," she said. "I never thought you were."

He moistened his lips. "I'm sorry I took my hand away from you, and I'm sorry I walked out on you like that."

She took his face in her hands and gave him a kiss. "My benediction. I hereby bestow upon you the honor of sainthood. Better?"

He responded with a long, lingering kiss.

"Will you pray with me?" he said.

They sat and prayed before heading out. They then walked along the river Tevere, and ended up in a Trattoria in the Trastevere area where they ate and laughed about a great many small things.

CHAPTER 41

FALLING IN LOVE

Marco had to keep his plan to go back to Venice the next day. He already had his return ticket, so he made certain to make his last night together with Genevieve in Rome as magical as they could. It was a mild evening, and the stars shone brightly. They sat by the side of the river counting the stars. They took long silent walks, holding hands, soaking up each other's presence to take with them. Their kisses took on an urgency that made it clear to them and any who saw them, that the love they had found was real and mutual. That night they lay wrapped in each other's arms. In the morning, they made love slowly and with a gravitas that belied their youth. After a small breakfast, Genevieve walked Marco to the train station.

"I hate to leave you behind," Marco told her. "I have so much I have to do, though. My first love is Venice, and that must remain, but in you, I know my soulmate. I pray we will not be apart for long." He held her hands in his as he professed his love.

"I will soon have time off from classes," Genevieve responded. "What do you think about me coming to Venice to see you then? It will only be a few days."

Marco lit up. "It will be the longest few days until I see you again, but I will take any time that you will give me."

Marco boarded the train, looked at Genevieve through the window, and they each raised a hand in loving salute as it pulled out of the station. He sat back thinking he would need to talk to Manin as soon as possible, and perhaps even talk with the Wizard of Tribuka. Somebody had to break this curse, and it fell on him to do that. He had never realized how falling in love would change him. He had always loved Venice. He had always wanted to save Venice, and he still did. But now he wanted to get Venice taken care of so that he could focus on building a life with his new love. As the train gently rocked from side to side moving down the tracks, Marco texted a poem to Genevieve called "The Gold Grass."

"How many days have passed?
How many times have you been
Immersed in the field of Love?
How many times has warm flesh
Excited your soul?
How many times
Did you reach the hills,
Where the grass is gold,
The sun is warm,
And your soul can melt in peace?
Times goes very fast,
Life never came back.
I want to go with you
Again, where the grass
Is gold forever."

Letting his newly found love wash over him like a healing balm, Marco remembered the feel of her arms, the taste of her kiss, like strawberries in spring. He could still smell her scent all over him and in his nose and in his head. He closed his eyes, and a familiar voice came to him in his dream: "It is me." That voice was so familiar. It was Morgana's. But was it Morgana or was it Genevieve? Could they possibly be the same person? Is it possible that Morgana transported and transformed herself in order to became Genevieve? As Marco's dream continued, he found himself running in fields of gold. Today the barley seemed even more golden. Maybe love on earth meant eternal love. Perhaps the very act of falling in love is enough to run free in the field of gold. He was smiling in his dreamy state, and finally, a woman appeared before him. But it was not Morgana; it was Genevieve. His Genevieve. They held hands, and they ran, and they rolled in the fields of gold.

CHAPTER 42

PUBLIC OUTCRY

He was brought out of his reverie when he heard someone on the train talking about "the young guy from the newspaper who had told off parliament." He was all over the local news and gossip of Rome.

"Foolish kid thought he could change parliament," a young man a few rows behind him said.

"Kudos to him for his courage," another one replied.

"Nah, he has to be crazy to bother with that bunch."

He searched the local news stories online. Some journalists were calling him a mythomaniac. Why didn't they just man up and call him a liar flat out? One accused him of blinded enthusiasm and naiveté. Another saw him as a spoiled kid, a representative of a rotten new generation. And another called him a hero for standing up to the complacent powers that be. All agreed that something had to be done for Venice. None agreed on how to do that. The press was no better than parliament in their lack of commitment.

Marco made up his mind: The public, with all its chatter, was on its own. It was just too much for him to deal with now and so he decided to leave it be. He laid his head back and began to rest in the warmth of Genevieve's memory when he got a text message.

"Nobody has ever written me a poem before! I love you so much and cannot wait to see you again!"

His heart soaring, he texted back: "I can't wait to see you this weekend. It's only Tuesday. I might go to pieces before then. But I'll show you the city that I love. And I will show my city the girl that I love."

She responded almost immediately, *"I will! I cannot wait! XXOO."*

He texted back with a heart emoji, settled into his seat, and drifted off to sleep smiling.

———

At home, the sight of Piazza San Marco, the statue of Manin, and his front door gladdened him. He was exhausted physically and mentally. Then his ears perked up at a sound from far off. It was the sound of pain, of lamentation.

He squinted, just able to discern movement and shapes all through the square around him on all sides.

Countless people, millions more than could have ever fit on the whole island, were on fire.

It burned through the skin, consuming no fuel, but leaving living torches in torment. A young man ran into the middle of the square. He dove and rolled, attempting to escape the flames, but they followed him, sticking to his skin like napalm. He was screaming. Marco tried to call out, but the young man was oblivious.

He looked behind him and saw a middle-aged woman lying on the ground in front of a home. She was on her back, hugging her knees, weeping. She rolled onto her side, to her back, onto her other side, and then onto her back again. She, unlike the young man, must have realized that no matter how hard she tried, evading the flames was impossible. Accepting the fact, she, unlike the young man, no longer tried to escape her fate. Thus, she lay in passive submission, pitifully rolling. She was not screaming, but every few seconds her eyes widened at the registration of a new shock of pain and she would gasp. Choking on air, she succumbed fully to her agony, tears gushing down her face. Marco felt pity and tried to call out to her, and the woman heard, but her resignation to her fate was without limit, and so she did not listen.

There were similar scenes all throughout the square. Some of the people had no eyes, only holes. At the same time, he saw their eyes scattered throughout the square, some trampled by fervent runners. He stood transfixed, unable to escape the horrific sight. Other people were, at that moment, tearing their own eyes out, as if they could release themselves from their suffering and the knowledge of the scene before them by escaping into darkness. However, their effort was in vain. Marco stood aghast.

He noticed then that the buildings surrounding the piazza were more pristine and beautiful than he had ever seen them—standing upright, as they had never had so much as a crack in their foundation in their lifetime. However, the piazza itself was full of people writhing and shrieking—blind, futile, and resigned. These people were so close Marco could reach out and touch them, only when he tried it, his hand passed right through them.

"Father," he prayed earnestly, "if there is any chance to save these people, I pray that you give me the strength to save them. Amen."

The fiery vision disappeared as quickly as it had come upon him with those words uttered.

Slowly he walked up to the statue of Manin. The statue appeared as it always had, but Marco realized that there was something more to the stoic expression of Manin. The man was in agony. The stoic expression of the statue merely a mask the statue had donned to hide his suffering.

There was no denying it anymore for Marco. It was like looking at a child trying to cover his face with his hands so that nobody sees that he is crying—a useless attempt to appear strong. Though the man's face was one of great suffering, he did not respond to Marco's words, nor did the lion.

"I got a small taste of what you must have had to deal with every day of your life," Marco told the statue. "I sat and observed parliament accomplish absolutely nothing, and for no good reason. I was so frustrated with them that I told them off for being colossal wastes of Italian time and resources. They told me I was lucky they didn't have me arrested. If someone doesn't hear the truth, then they must be living a lie." He looked down. "I told them the truth." He looked back up at Manin, "I didn't get one good thing done for Venice. What should I do? Can you talk to me now?"

The statue of Manin remained frozen. There was not even a shudder, no indication whatsoever that he heard Marco. Marco was dumbfounded. It was almost as if the statue had never come alive at all. Had he imagined their whole conversation? Was he going crazy? Did Tribuka freeze Manin in his world in the other dimension and now was coming to take Venice?

He went home, staring at the ground as he walked.

———

The next morning his father threw the paper down before him.

"These people are not getting your message," he said. "They think you are crazy. I don't want them to hurt you."

Marco hugged his father. "Papa, you know that anyone who has ever made the world better was called crazy for their vision. But I'm harmless to them. But they just feel a little uncomfortable because they know I am speaking the truth."

"That is precisely the harm they see in you and precisely the reason I'm worried."

"I met a girl, Papa."

The man looked at his son, a wry smile on his face. "You did?"

"She is the one."

His father waved a dismissive hand. "All the more reason to be careful, for now your judgment is compromised."

Every turn, a brick wall—first the Venetian people, then parliament, and now his own father.

———

At University the next day, Marco was sitting at his desk writing when one of the jocks pounded his fist on the table.

"You make us Venetians look crazy!" said the brute.

Marco stared him down. "And you make us look disgusting. I've seen you pissing in the canal. Don't talk to me if you can't take pride in your city." Marco continued staring into the student's eyes until the bully looked down and walked away.

As he gathered his books to leave, he heard other students laughing behind his back. It was refreshing to be able to put a bully in his place, but he knew it was only a minor victory that only served to remind him of how frustrating his attempts had been to get help in Rome. It was a good thing that his appointment with the mayor was that day. He needed perspective. He was worried he might do something rash in his next encounter. He was too emotional to be circumspect at the moment, and he knew it.

CHAPTER 43

FOCUS BACK ON VENICE

The Mayor's secretary came out from behind her desk and wrapped Marco in a motherly embrace. "You poor thing!" she said, as she backed away a little to look him in the eyes, still holding onto his shoulders. "Remember, all great men have been through this, Marco. You will go through it, too. You may take note of the journalists who saw your courage and your intelligence and your compassion. But also take note of criticism that doesn't use flowery language or rhetoric. Those who criticize without an agenda are your friends. Everyone else just wants to sell papers and don't care about what's true or what's good."

"Thank you," he said. "Thank you for seeing through all the lies and confusion, and for seeing me for who I am and for what I'm doing." He smiled shyly. "I've wanted to tell someone this, but I haven't been able to yet. I met my twin flame in Rome. She's coming this weekend to see Venice for the first time. I think God sent her to keep me from buckling under all this pressure."

"Oh, how lovely!" the secretary squealed in joy. "I am so happy for you, Marco! I hope to meet this lucky young lady." Marco promised he would introduce them and sauntered into the mayor's office.

"You were a better man than I was the first time I went to Parliament," said Ongaro. "After all, you didn't wind up in jail. But my story is for another time. I am proud of you, Marco. I sent you to learn, and you learned. I'm sorry, where are my manners, please take a seat." The Mayor gestured toward a leather armchair by his desk while he took the opposite one.

"I understand why you said what you did," the mayor continued. "Now tell me, how close did your words get you to accomplish your goal?"

Marco looked at the floor, ashamed. "They probably got me farther away from my goals," he said. "I was so angry I couldn't believe that they could dismiss tens of thousands of lives over a petty bureaucratic rule!"

"Parliaments do that all the time. It's practically their *raison d'etre*. It's a horrible fact of life that they must stick to the rules even when the rules cause damage. But if they break the rules for a worthy cause, the next time it will be for one that is not so worthy, and that is the slippery slope of governance. It's worse than corruption. And when your government doesn't care whether you know about their corruption, it is because they know you have no power to change things anymore. And that's when they own you. Neither of us is in a position of power over them, at least not yet. So tell me, what could you have done to get Venice the help she needs?"

"That's just it. There was nothing I could do or say to make a difference. I figured that at least if I told them off, they might have the sense to hear and to know I was right. But that didn't work either, so I guess there was no point in my being there."

The mayor smiled and put a reassuring hand on his young friend's arm.

"There was a critical point in your being there, Marco," the mayor said. "First, people are now talking about Venice. Venice's needs are in the front of everybody in Italy's mind right now. Sure, it's in the context of the 'crazy' kid who yelled at parliament, but I can assure you that over 90 percent of Italians would love to give parliament a piece of their mind. They may call you crazy, but secretly they wish they could do the same. Still, it is time to plan and act. What might you do in the future to help get parliament to vote on this important issue?"

"I should probably build friendships with deputies," Marco said with resignation. "If they get to know me they'll take me seriously. But I don't think we have time."

"We may not have time," the mayor said. "But we've got to work as if we did within the political world while taking using any expedients we have. There is something else you can do. Can you think of what it is?"

"Your secretary suggested that I befriend the journalists who took me seriously," Marco replied.

"And that I take note of who criticized me without an agenda."

Ongaro smiled. "She's been hanging around me too long. That is precisely the advice I was going to give you."

After a few pleasantries about the weather in Rome, Marco was standing up to go when the mayor bade him to sit back down. "Why the rush, my young friend? You have happy news to share with me, I can see it in your bearing. You're practically bouncing in the seat, even when you feel terrible. Am I not worthy to share your joy as well as your pain?"

"You're worthy." He felt his face blaze. "I've met the girl of my dreams, the one I'm going to marry."

The Mayor's eyes lit up, and his whole face broke into a broad smile. "You met the most beautiful girl in the world and she forgot her glasses?"

"Well, if she did, I hope she never finds them because she seems to like me just fine, too."

"Allow me," the mayor said, and called on his secretary to procure a bottle of Prosecco. "If we cannot toast newfound romance, then there is nothing in the world we can toast. Oh, but one more thought. Do you know how you will be able to tell a fool when you see one today?"

Marco shook his head.

"He will talk badly about you and what you did in Rome," the mayor continued. "You were not expected to respond perfectly at parliament. If you had, I would have been surprised and frankly disappointed. You needed to learn what you've been learning from that frustrating experience. You needed to yell at those stupid old men. You needed to take your passion to a bigger world and get ignored or worse, because you have the potential for greatness in you, and without those setbacks, you could never get there. I am sorry I could not prepare you. I had to throw you to the sharks, as they say."

When the bottle arrived, they toasted love first, and then fate.

CHAPTER 44

FOOL PLAY

Later, walking off campus, Marco pulled out his cell phone and called the local newspaper. It was time to meet with the journalist nearest him. They made plans to meet for coffee the next day, at the same cafe that the mayor preferred.

Marco decided to take a long walk and see all of Venice again. Despite the mayor's reassurances, he still felt like he was losing his city. He was grieving much as a man might grieve a dying parent. It was midday, and the sun flooded the city making everything look warm and welcoming. The rays were reflecting off Ca' D'oro. It was aptly named, reflecting the sunlight as it did. He went to the Rialto Bridges and walked down to Campo San Bartolomeo, proceeding toward St Mark square. Then he decided to walk back toward his home and to the Accademia and Campo San Barnaba. He arrived at the train station and took a part of the Lista di Spagna, then turned into the Jewish ghetto. He passed the old synagogue, remembering the one time he went in. He was at a wedding of one of his friends and had to wear a yarmulke. He still had the photograph of his friend smiling proudly and in love and Marco next to him looking like a young Torah student.

Past the synagogue he found himself in the main square with the restaurants all around and the bridge at the end. The house was colorful and well kept. He was staring at the restaurant owned by his friend Viviana. She was not there. After the Jewish wedding, the reception was in her restaurant. There he'd had multiple types of fish, but for the first time, he tasted wine from Israel, which was like tasting Scripture itself. He still preferred Italian wine.

From there, he went into the fondamente Della Misericordia, up to the arsenale and took the back street to St. Elena. He sat at St. Elena. He had been walking quite a while and decided to take the vaporetto to the Basilica of the Madonna Della Pieta. He stopped in the church and prayed for Venice and Genevieve. Then he walked to the point of the island where a golden angel shows the direction of the wind, and then looking at the canal Della Giudeca to the Zattere. There he stopped. He was tired. Tables were out. The sun was reflecting on all the buildings, including the Molino Stucky on the other side of the canal. He could see Marghera Port in the distance. He sat at a table and ordered a gelato. The day was ending, and he wanted to collect his thoughts. While sitting, he saw a few tourist boats pass in front of him. The people waved at him, smiling. They seemed happy to be there.

At the cafe, Marco noticed a journalist he knew, a man by the name of Paolo, seated nearby. He asked if he could join him. Paolo was not much older than Marco and they had met a few times at the paper, but only in passing. He explained to Paolo the UNESCO project, the goals and the discussions in parliament. He explained his frustration and why he had his outburst. Paolo was a serious journalist. He listened impartially, asked probing questions designed to get to the heart of the matter, and he was fair in his reporting. Paolo had some perspectives of his own to offer

Marco, telling him about his own early experiences of being frustrated by parliament.

Marco told Paolo about the legends of Venice that fathers used to pass to their children. He told the journalist about meeting the old man in Burano and how he had learned so much from him. He talked about how the stories vanished during the mid-twentieth century, and the generations since have been deprived of those stories. He asked Paolo if he could get them published in the newspaper. Paolo was intrigued. He said he felt confident that he could get them in the paper and told Marco to email them to him.

As they parted, Marco thought he had a new friend and a possible ally.

CHAPTER 45

THE RAIN

The next day at the university, Marco ignored the name-calling and the sneers. They no longer mattered. He had taken the mayor's advice to heart, and his skin was thicker for it.

The day was colder than the previous day had been. He was surprised at the sudden cold weather in the middle of the Indian summer, but the weather app on his phone indicated good weather through the weekend. He was glad to know Genevieve would have good weather for their first time in Venice together.

That night he received a text from Genevieve. *"I can't make it Friday for the weekend, but I can come in Sunday and stay a week. Is that okay?"*

He texted back, "It will be two days longer of missing you, but I will gladly take the week with you. Come to me when you can. I love you."

She responded, *"I can't wait! I love you too!"* and then the phone went silent.

Marco was left with his thoughts, but the sound of the TV in the other room interfered with his reverie.

His father was in the family room watching TV. Marco listened as the weatherman warned of an atmospheric perturbation coming in from the North. This was a sudden change. Those wheatear apps never work well, he thought. The rain was so violent and impetuous that after one hour the Canales were already filled up. Marco got his raincoat and high boots on and went out.

The water had been rising from the incessant rain. The people were on edge.

"Move! I have to go first. I am in a hurry!"

"Hey, old man give me your umbrella. You don't need it since you are going to die soon anyhow."

"Hey, fat lady, move aside. You are taking up the entire calle."

Insults hurled like tiny projectiles all over the city. Some got violent at the slightest provocation. They feared something catastrophic, but couldn't name it.

Venice had always had high tides, but nobody could remember the last time it had rained this much. Marco walked around the city through the rain, hoping it would stop. He was shocked when the people he met on his walk were rude to him.

"Ragazzo, what you doing out? Don't you think you should be with your mammy?"

It was as if rain made people forget their sense of decency. He looked out at it, touched it. What kind of rain was this that would turn a population into crude ruffians? He tried ambling down the more secluded streets, hoping to sink into his thoughts, but the rain kept interrupting his solitude. Annoyed, exhausted, and wet, he went back home, dried off, and fell asleep.

"Welcome back, boy! Captain Willem van der Decken at your service!"

Marco opened his eyes and looked around. He was back aboard the Flying Dutchman. Looking abeam to port, he could only see dark thunderclouds and a black, swirling sea. It was anxious, violent, and hungry.

"We have come for you boy! We are back for you, ready to give you a ride with our lady of the sea to provide you with safe passage over these 'ere waters." The Captain bowed deeply. "You did well, but I fear you've discovered that people are people. You cannot always count on them. They're always focused on their ghosts! Little do they know we're the only ghosts around here." He erupted in a hearty laugh. "What a life for them and us—them, always running away from their ghosts—and us, always chasing them! Well may be ghosts, but at least we're at peace. People are born, and they die, but we are always here reminding them of the lives they could have lived and the lives they still can have. That gives us all the peace we need."

Marco thought for a moment. "What do you mean by *waters*? What are you talking about?"

"Listen, lad," the Captain said, his tone becoming grave, "your people had a lot of chances to change, but they refused to. And now, they're going to get what's coming to them. Some will be hurt who don't deserve it, others *will* deserve it, but no one is coming out of this unscathed. Not even you, Marco." He paused. "But lucky for you, you have this fine vessel to carry you to safety!" Again, he let out his hearty laugh.

"But Signor Captain, can't you be merciful? Can't you just help them to change?"

"'Tis not me what's brought this fate upon them. They brought it upon themselves. I've tried my best to warn them, but it is difficult to change who you are. At a certain point, no matter how hard you try, there's still going to be something about yourself you can't change. Sometimes I don't want to be Captain van der Decken, but it's who I am and who I will be for eternity." He paused again and smiled. "But as far as ghost lives go, I live a pretty decent one." At that, he laughed joyfully and without scorn.

Marco did not know if he should laugh too or if he should be worried.

"Well, with that, my friend, I bid you adieu!"

The captain took off his hat and bowed with a flourish.

Before Marco could do the same, his vision went black.

———

He awoke with sunlight streaming through his window and the light of reason beginning to enter his mind. He read that morning's paper with eagerness. Paolo had been fair and had told both sides of the story as best he could. He explained how Marco had been frustrated at parliament and why. He described the delayed vote and the reason for it. He reached out to the deputies, but none returned his calls, and he reported that, too. He made particular note of the fact that a citizen has every right to call out his deputies when they don't do their jobs. Marco was thrilled with the article.

Then he looked in the arts and society section of the paper to find his story of the Wizard of Tribuka. Paolo had interviewed old men around Venice to discover the legend. He had also written about how the legends had been shared from father to son for generations up until World War II. He signed off with the promise of more legends of Venice.

As Marco finished reading the paper, the high tide sirens sounded, a strange occurrence for September. The rain fell steadily for hours on end. Weather forecasters could not explain the heavy clouds over Venice.

Saturday morning, the tide was at five feet. Some footbridges were barely above water, others were completely covered. The national and international news was now discussing meteorological changes around Venice with a variety of theories ranging from global warming to a meteor strike near the city.

It was clear that none of them had any idea what they were talking about.

It was reported that tourists had been cleared off the islands already and residents were beginning to worry. Furthermore, the beach in Lido was now fully submerged. The civil protection chief ordered a total evacuation of the sandbar. There was a long line of cars packed high inside and outside with luggage and food, all tied up with any type of rope they could find and covered with plastic. Panic rached its peak at the ferry that was supposed to take them back to the mainland. At one point, people left their cars on the side of the street in order to escape to the mainland.

Thunderstorms had never lasted very long, and high tide had never looked like this. The bits of conversation were quoted: The apocalypse, a denial of the peculiarity of the situation, Marco's letters and the tail of the wizard.

Everywhere Marco went, people stopped him for advice. He told them all the same thing, "If it's not too late, start taking care of Venice. It's nothing I haven't said already."

"And what if it *is* too late?" a woman asked him.

Marco looked at her and said, "That's when it's time to pray."

Marco was frustrated. If everyone started working together, the city could be saved, but by this point, hope was nothing more than a Fata Morgana mirage. Even so, he still went around to talk to people, but they were all too scared and his words went unheard. Fear was taking control. Hearts and minds were sinking right along with the city.

After talking to many of the residents of the city, Marco began to make his way to city hall. He needed to discuss with Ongaro how to meet the present situation and how to assuage the fears of the citizens.

Marco arrived at the building and went inside. There was no receptionist in the entry hall. There was no one anywhere.

He walked down the hallway toward the mayor's office and met no secretaries, no interns. No one greeted him except the sound of raised voices coming from the end of the hall in the direction of the mayor's office. He finally arrived at the room where he and the mayor had had so many meetings.

There he found Ongaro surrounded by at least twenty other city officials. All of them were yelling at each other and at him. The mayor was too overwhelmed with the cascades of phone calls to indulge in the shouting match. Through the shouting, Marco heard parts of plans for how the city should keep as many people safe as possible. The Mayor slammed his fist on the desk, and all went quiet.

"We will give the order for a total evacuation of Venice!" He was panting from the stress as he locked eyes with Marco. Shame took over his face.

No words were needed. It was over. And Marco returned home.

CHAPTER 46

VENETIAN PALADINS AND HELL FOR THE VENETIAN

Marco arrived at the square where he lived and found it deserted.

"Marco, what you are doing strolling like that? Come on!"

It was his father.

"We need to go right now! We've packed everything!"

Marco looked at his father. "Papa, I cannot." He was surprised to find his own voice as resolute as his gait. "I have to stay. Please believe me. I *need* to stay. If Venice changes, it will be because of me. You see, everything that I have been saying is true. It was all true. Now the people, believe me, Papa. They finally all believe me! Please hear me."

"Marco, if you stay here, you will drown! You'll die! The whole city is sinking, don't you see? Stop dreaming for once in your life! There is no changing Venice. She is doomed. No one can save her now."

"Papa," Marco said indignantly, "it is *exactly* that attitude that brought Venice to this point. Don't you realize that everyone has refused to take responsibility for Venice, justifying themselves by saying, 'Venice is going to be dirty anyway? We don't need to clean it. There are no Venetians who live here anymore. There's no need to reclaim our home.' Remember when you said that there's no point in improving the floodgates because Venice is going to sink under all the tourists eventually? Well, here we are, Papa. That day has come."

"You're right Marco. Venice's day has come, and it's our day to leave."

"No! I have never abandoned Venice before, and I don't plan on doing it now. You're worried I will die, but I know I won't be able to live with myself if I abandoned my home."

"You can't fight the sea, Marco! It's hopeless!"

"Then I will provide hope! Don't you see? All this is happening because we *lost* our hope. Hope is the enemy of destruction. And if my hope is the last Venice will ever see, then I will die having fought fitfully."

Papa choked back a sob as he hugged his son harder than he ever had before. "I understand Marco. I am sorry that I did not believe in you as much as I should have. I love you very much. I don't want to lose you, but you wouldn't be Marco if you abandoned your passion." He hugged his son again and said, "I've never been prouder to be your father."

"Look, even under all this water, even with this bad weather," added Marco, pointing at the window. "Venice is still beautiful."

They remained like that, embracing each other for a long time. Finally, his father stepped back, away from Marco, took a deep breath, and whispered in his ear, "I will tell your mother that you will catch another boat and meet us later. She would never agree to allow you to stay here, but I understand, and I apologize for not having done more."

"Just do all that you can right now," Marco whispered back so his mother could not hear. "Save mother. Don't worry about me. I will see you soon." He tried to smile. They hugged again. Marco went in and hugged his mother as well. And then he watched his parents scurry away behind the corner.

He had to get himself to the statue of Manin. He waded through the water in the square in his high boots to the foot of the statue. When he looked up, the statue was stepping down. Manin signaled to the roof of the house by Marco's bedroom window. Marco understood and went back into the house, up to his room, and out his bedroom window just in time to see Manin dismounting from the lion. Marco sat next to Manin, the lion shielding them from the rain as they talked. He realized that Manin was now a man of human skin. The rain had washed away his bronze.

"We lost, Marco," Manin said sadly. "It was inevitable. We were doomed, and now the end is here."

Marco's tears burned in the cold rain. He felt like a total failure.

"Marco," Manin continued, "You were the authentic son of Venice. I could not be prouder of you if you were my own true son. You have fought to the very end. You have stood up for love, for beauty, and for Venice. Never think you failed. The Wizard of Tribuka was right. Man cannot keep beautiful things, as we are incapable of caring enough.

"I did not expect we would perish like this. So many good men laid down their lives for Venice. I thought that the courageous act would count for more. But it is too late to cast blame. Nothing will save Venice now. She will sink beneath the waves until the Wizard sees enough love in the souls that remain. That could be a very long time indeed. Until man learns to search his soul, we are doomed."

Manin stopped ruminating for a moment and fixed a look of intense concern upon Marco. "Your calling is far from over, my friend. The wizard has said that your bravery and intelligence have caused him to give you this offer. He will spare you and all those you love from eternal slavery if you travel the world telling everybody about how Venice was destroyed by apathy and laziness and human indifference. You are to survive this cataclysm so that you can teach people to love more deeply, to care more fully—otherwise they will come to an end no better than this one."

Awestruck, Marco found he could neither speak nor move.

"The wizard is just beginning," continued Manin. "He will take Venice tonight, but one day the God of all will start punishing them even before He comes again. God will take their most precious thing—their eternal souls will be dammed for eternity."

Marco had lost all sense of time. It was well past midnight, the sky black as pitch without a single star to be seen. He couldn't imagine evacuations still happening with the water almost at his feet now, and he was two stories above the ground.

"It is time to go," Manin said, breaking Marco from his trance. "Come with me."

Manin stood and reached for Marco's hand. Marco took it and stood. Manin gestured that he should climb on the lion's back, and so he did. Manin got on the lion's back behind him, and the lion stood up, unfurled its wings, and flew off the roof well above the rising waters.

Beneath them, the water was coming in waves, and the waves were getting taller and taller. The time between crests gave the water enough time to drown all the buildings and people it could find. More than a tsunami, it looked like a humongous beast with an open mouth that devoured everything in his path.

"From atop the basin of Piazza San Marco," Manin told Marco, "I want to show you something. Watch the foundation wall of the town."

As Marco looked at the wall, it began to crumble under the weight of the water. He heard screams and cries, people begging to be saved. There were people trying to ride the waves, but they were sucked into the whirlpool of water. Others tried to reach for the closest boat only to have it capsize on them, and they disappeared beneath it.

Marco knew that evacuating a city could not be easy. People can be stubborn and don't want to leave behind their belongings, their home, their life. They would try to stay in the abandoned city hoping all would just go away. There was no more contempt in him, only pity.

Sounds of human desperation died quickly as Marco watched more and more people sweep under the water along with the land they had been standing on.

"Every one of those people had made their pact with the wizard," Manin told him. "He now owns their souls in exchange for a life they did not care enough about. They traded their souls for apathy, and now they are damned forever. Behold!"

Marco looked and saw hundreds of dead bloated bodies floating out to what had been the grand canal.

"Those are the ones who talked but never took action," Manin said. "They were like inflated balloons, blown up with hot air and doing nothing. Their last breaths inflated with water."

As they continued to fly onward, Manin told Marco to look to his left.

"Those people are vomiting worms. Those were the powermongers who used law and custom to maintain their power without thought of service. That is their eternal punishment. And look, see those few dozens sitting peacefully on the only dry land left? Those are the Paladins of Venice. They fought for her, each in their way, just as you did. They are waiting patiently, knowing they did all they could. Transport will come for them soon, and they will return to the mainland to continue their lives, to fight for goodness, as you will."

Marco recognized the mayor, the young journalist Paolo, and others he knew among the crowd.

"There," Manin said, pointing up ahead. "Those people will be sweeping the streets of water for all eternity. They never fought for Venice. They never loved her. They defiled and demeaned her all of their days, and now they are doomed to clean her for all eternity."

Marco was not surprised to see the bully from school the other day among them.

"Finally," said Manin, "you can see the ones eating the earth at their feet. They filled their pockets with gold, fame, and finery at the expense of others. Their rapacious greed has always left them hungry. Now they can gorge themselves on mud. Is it worth much more than gold to them now?"

The lion suddenly surged upward. The wind was rushing past his face trying to throw him off, but he held onto the lion. When they leveled off, he could see that Lido was no more. The lagoon no longer existed either. There was only the sea, and it was hungrily devouring the island city.

"I must leave you now," said Manin. "I will sit with the Paladins and wait to be saved. Everyone who fought for Venice in her whole history is alive in another dimension. We are the Paladins. We are few, but we are strong. I met everyone a long time ago before my exile in Tribuka, but I know they are there among the people, there are but a few in Tribuka and others in a different part of the Universe—all are ready to fight. You are a Paladin now. Welcome, and may you be full of faith that one day Venice will return to her splendor."

"Tell me more about these Paladins, Signore Manin. Give me some hope, please."

"I cannot say much, but I can assure you that many people who fought for Venice were kept alive and hidden by Merlin and Morgana in case a disaster bringing about the end of Venice were to occur. Merlin was wise, as he knew that most humans never change. Tribuka discovered this, and I had to become his slave in exchange for other people keeping their identities hidden.

"You must stay on the lion for now. This is how you will survive. The wizard is coming and the end is near. He will take Venice with him to another dimension where he will carefully rebuild it to its original glory, but for his enchantment. As each worthy Venetian dies, their soul will return to Venice to live in peace forever in that new dimension. I will see you again."

A clap of thunder interrupted Manin's talking. Marco quickly realized that it wasn't a clap of thunder, it was the thundering laughter of the Wizard of Tribuka.

"Man is not a good animal," said a voice from the clouds. "I thought you could learn through wars and pestilence, but the lessons only lasted for a generation or two. I had hopes that you could change. You've disappointed me. I have been waiting for this moment for centuries upon centuries. Now, at last, Venice is mine to add to my collection of beautiful things your world had but was not worthy of. The library at Alexandria, Lemuria, and Atlantis is already there, along with the Garden of Eden. I have known for a very long time that humans will not take care of what is theirs." The Wizard let out a roaring laugh.

The lion touched down next to the Paladins, and Manin got off its back.

CHAPTER 47

THE APOCALYPSE

The lion took to the air again as another of the wizard's laughs engulfed the area. A tsunami was now moving quickly toward the basin of Piazza San Marco. Water engulfed St. Helena and then the area of the Arsenale, where the old Venetians were building their boats. Then the Rialto Bridge went under. The water took the Palazzo Ducale and the tower of San Marco. The giant wave heaved toward the university and back to the Misericordia site. It tore through the Jewish ghetto to the train and bus stations. The tsunami slammed back and forth, creating more wreckage the longer it moved. It swallowed the Zattere.

Marco could not see any more buildings. There was no sign of land for many miles.

As dawn broke, the clouds receded, and the waters calmed. The first rays of sun shone on the peaceful Adriatic Sea where a city had stood not twenty-four hours earlier. In the distance, he saw Marghera Port, where people were still arriving by boat from Venice to go to Mestre. Nothing else was left.

Venice was gone.

Nobody who had missed that last boat had survived.

All of a sudden, something moved from the closest boat to his. From below three dead bodies, a living cat scrambled up. Only one of the million cats from Venice had survived. It was an Egyptian Bastet, which legend said was the reincarnation of the goddess. She was known as the goddess of perfume and ointment, at that time as valuable as gold since those commodities were essential in the process of mummification.

But why was this cat here? Just then, Marco remembered that Bastet was also considered the goddess of warfare. That made Marco hopeful since the war had just begun. The imperative now was that no one, not even a cat, should give up the battle with Tribuka. Leaning down from the back of the lion, Marco worked his way close to the boat and scooped the cat into his hands. It was a little kitten, maybe 4-6 weeks old.

"Hello, little one," he said. "If you survived such a tsunami, you are a warrior and you should be with me. I'll call you Bastet. Stay here now." A little sign of life in the middle of the death. In any other circumstance, cats were the one thing Marco had never been able to stand, since they were everywhere in Venice, like an infestation. But here was a miracle cat that he would make his companion.

The persistent sounds of screaming, panic, and the tortured un-dead remained in Marco's head.

"Dear God," Marco muttered to himself as his eyes remained wide open in horror. "We have killed our beloved city. The thing I feared most has now happened."

He felt a lump rise in his throat. The lion took Marco down to the water where a small boat with two oars floated gently. He jumped off the lion's back and into the boat. He watched as the lion looked him in the eye, bowed his head in respect, and flew off through the clouds. His mission was complete.

Marco picked up the oars, placed them in the oarlocks and began rowing toward the mainland. The more he rowed, the deeper his grief became. With the first stroke of the oars, the lump in his throat burst, and tears started flowing down his cheeks in a constant stream. He rowed with greater intensity as he felt his heart release years of fear, grief, frustration, and now, horror. He rowed toward the coast, every stroke of the oars bringing him closer to healing the ancient agony he had carried with him from many past lives of loving Venice. He thought about the Buddhists and the Hindus who believe in reincarnation and felt bitter. Marco shouted, "And how is that supposed to work? I don't suppose reincarnation works for cities, does it?" His voice broke. "There's no way Venice can come back to life now." He began to sob bitterly. "I want my Venice back with all its defects. I just want it back..."

Finally, he couldn't take it anymore and stopped rowing. He yelled until his vocal cords could produce no more sound. Then he fell into the bottom of the boat, curled into a fetal position, and sobbed until he had no more tears left. Then he lay there, his gaze directed at the wall of the boat but looking at nothing.

There was a change in the air. He felt it. And it made him sit up.

He looked out on the horizon and began to make out the shape of Venice again.

"She is coming back," he yelled. "Venice is coming back!"

"Believe in me, Marco."

Marco recognized the familiar voice as that of Morgana.

"Your people destroyed Venice," she continued. "But we can rebuild her. You have to find the Paladin. They exist among the people of the earth. Find them and unite them. Find them and unite them. *Believe... me...*"

Marco, exhausted, fainted in his boat.

⸺

He awoke to the rapid thrumming of helicopters, the kitten licking his face and kneading his chest with her tiny claws. He had no idea how long he had slept, but he knew precisely where he was.

As he heard the helicopters coming closer, he saw something pop up to float on the water. It was a body. Then another popped up. Then another and another until the entire sea around Marco's little boat was littered with human bodies. He started to row as fast as he could to get out of this sea of corpses. Bastet, frightened, tucked her squat body beneath his legs. Marco's oars bounced off the bodies, moving them aside. But there were so many covering every inch of water that Marco could no longer see the water around him. And soon he could no longer row because his oars were stuck, caught on the limbs of one of the corpses.

One body rolled face up, and Marco recognized his friend Giorgio. He gasped at the sight. He bent over the edge of the boat to kiss his friend on the forehead, and then pulled the shirt at the shoulder, trying to bring the body into the boat so that he could give him a proper burial. But Giorgio's shirt tore and he slipped from Marco's hands. It then sunk slowly into the murky waters.

The corpse having sunk, its place at the surface was replaced by others. Marco's hand was still extended, but there was nothing more to reach for. He withdrew his hand, took a deep breath, said a prayer for Giorgio's soul, and continued rowing, trying to break through this sea of bodies.

"Oh! There's Philip," he shouted out loud. His mask maker friend who had moved to Venice from the English Riviera. Marco did not even know if Phil had believed in God or not, but he said a prayer for him, too.

When he finished, without even realizing what it was he was saying, he uttered, "We had everything before us. Now we have nothing before us. We are bound for hell."

Hours must have passed when he finally landed at the dock of St. Giuliano's, the rowing society. People were everywhere. Many had dropped dead. But others floated above the city. Nobody had escaped destiny. As Marco stepped out of the boat, people surrounded him, but they did not talk. They reached out tentatively to touch him. They treated him like he was a Messiah. He was too stunned to react. He picked up Bastet in his arm.

"Marco, Marco, over here." It was Genevieve. She quickly explained to Marco that she had arrived earlier, but she was not allowed to go to Venice. All of the trains and the busses had stopped in Mestre. She had waited all night to see him. Marco had told her that the Wizard's curse would leave him unharmed, but she did not believe it until now.

Genevieve held him in her arms, caressing his head with her hand, crying. He stood there in her embrace with his arms by his side, his mouth agape, his eyes still wide open in horror. The crowd was getting thicker, and the people were looking at him expectantly, silently, as if they were waiting for him to say something.

Many people were on the lagoon shore—many faces, many souls. Nobody was talking. What was there to say? Marco was lost and confused. He wished he was among those who died, but instead he had to bear the burden of being a survivor. He was terrified, his body shaking. Genevieve felt it, and Marco could sense she did not know how to console him. Nothing could replace Venice for him. Genevieve must have understood that.

He looked around at the crowd, saying nothing.

"At best, this was the apocalypse," she said, finally. She quietly drew him towards her, hugged and tried to console him.

"Marco?" she asked softly with tears building in the corners of her eyes. He was still staring in shock at the spot of water that used to be his home. "Marco? Speak to me." He looked at her, still unable to speak. "Marco, I'm here for you. I'm still here, Marco. And who is this little beauty?" she said, picking up the kitten.

"She is Bastet... just Bastet," he said in a soft voice, still hoarse from yelling earlier. He looked at Genevieve.

"Yes, Marco? What is it?"

"I... don't... "

She hugged him close again and caressed his neck. "It's okay, Marco, I understand. You don't have to say anything. Don't be so adamant."

Marco's brows furrowed, and he whispered, "Adamant? That sounds familiar. A-da-man..." Then his eyes widened like he suddenly remembered something. "Paladin! Morgana! Paladin! Get back to Venice," he whispered.

Genevieve smiled confusedly at him, "What?"

"The Paladins!" he repeated louder. Genevieve tilted her head, but before she could ask him what he meant he continued. "There's still hope! The Paladins are still alive! Venice can still come back! It might be a small chance, but there's a chance!"

He looked at Genevieve with a weary smile and what must have been a crazed look in his eyes, as he told her. "Genevieve, stay with me and hope with me. If there's even a little bit of hope, I'll chase after it. If it's possible to bring Venice back, *we* will make it happen. You, me, Manin, the Paladins, all of us!" He grabbed her shoulders and laughed until tears came.

"Marco you're scaring me," she said.

Bastet had settled at his feet and was staring up with a quizzical expression.

"Genevieve, don't you see? There's still hope."

He felt it now inside him, beginning like a small fire. It was only a matter of love and time before it fanned into something that could evaporate all this water. But that was it. That was the solution. He had said it himself so many times, but his own passion had shielded him from the true light. Love and time. And now, hope, true hope. He could almost see the top of the tallest house begin to rise above the surface. Almost.

They kissed as only those who are truly in love could kiss. Then he stared into her eyes for a moment.

Yes, it was there. Venice was rising in her.

THE END